MW00396032

"Let me know when ready," West said. "No hurry."

Tammy nodded and turned back to her board. West knew Ben would have the scout ships fanning out around the bubble and standing by.

If they didn't set off detonations to pop the bubble at exactly the same time , whatever was inside would be crushed.

"Scanning distance," James said. "All stop."

"Scans started," Cynthia said from directly behind him. She was in charge of all scans of Void Space Bubbles. She was married and had two kids onboard and her husband was one of the lead scout pilots who set the explosives. She might be the shortest human on the entire ship at four-foot-three. But wow was she powerful.

Silence filled the command center as everyone waited.

At least until Cynthia said, "Oh, shit."

That was the first time West had ever heard her swear.

RESCUE TWO

ALSO BY DEAN WESLEY SMITH

THE SEEDERS UNIVERSE

Dust and Kisses: A Seeders Universe Prequel Novel

Against Time

Sector Justice

Morning Song

The High Edge

Star Mist

Star Rain

Star Fall

Starburst

Rescue Two

RESCUE TWO

A SEEDERS UNIVERSE SHORT NOVEL

DEAN WESLEY SMITH

Rescue Two

First published in *Smith's Monthly Issue #60,* April 2022
Published by WMG Publishing

ISBN-13 (trade paperback): 978-1-56146-725-9
ISBN-13 (hardcover): 978-1-56146-748-8

"Shadow in the City"

Based on the song lyrics of "Here in the City" by Janis Ian, written with permission for *Stars Anthology* edited by Janis Ian and Mike Resnick. The lyrics this story is based on are reprinted here with permission from Janis Ian.
First published in *Smith's Monthly Issue #39,* WMG Publishing, December 2016

"A Matter for a Future Year"

First published in *Stories from July,* WMG Publishing, July 2015

AUTHOR'S NOTE

Small parts of this novel were originally published as Seeders Universe short stories.

PROLOGUE

The oldest man on the Seeder ship *Lost Sense* sat alone in a room.

A loud burp cut through the room.

"Sorry," he said.

He said it to no one, since he was alone in the ship and had been now for over two hundred years. He commanded, was the Chairman of, and the only passenger of, the *Lost Sense*. The ship was big enough to house fifty crew, but easy enough for one to manage, so he and the others had decided only he would risk his own life on this mission.

His name was Larry Estrabrook.

He stood six-foot-two, had dark brown hair that was still thick, and muscles in his shoulders he worked on regularly.

As a Seeder, he had lived just over four thousand years and was part of the group of humans who were long-lived and were planning to spread humanity to other galaxies, just as they had done to many planets in the First Galaxy.

He knew a couple other Seeders who were older than he was, but he still liked to think of himself as the oldest man in just about any world and on any ship in any segment of the First Galaxy.

The Seeders called themselves Seeders because of the idea of not only seeding other planets with humans, but seeding other galaxies as well. It had seemed like a great idea at the time, although Larry had no idea what loony person had come up with it.

A galaxy was damn big and it took a hundred years to just get across the spiral First Galaxy. Why did they think they could seed other planets in other galaxies?

But not only did Seeders live a long time, it seems most of them thought of big ideas as well. Like this mission he was on. He was going to be the first Seeder to travel to another galaxy.

His mission was to test a new ship, new engine, and try to make it to the nearest satellite galaxy from the First Galaxy.

When in the new galaxy, he was also supposed to scout the small cluster galaxy and look for any sign of aliens. Seeders didn't want to mess with aliens.

The small cluster galaxy he was headed for was by far the closest to home and it was still going to take a four-hundred-year trip.

And if they were depending on him to send back information about the small galaxy, it looked like they might have to wait some more years beyond his scheduled arrival.

He was stuck.

Yup, stuck.

No idea how a spaceship could get stuck in the emptiness of space between galaxies, but he had managed it.

He was supposed to be in deep sleep for most of the four-hundred-year trip, but alarm systems had rousted him about two hundred years in.

Lost Sense was basically dead in a weird area of space. He couldn't see anything past the edge of whatever he had run into. His deep-space drive didn't work even though it was still in top condition, so he was going to have to use his sub-light-system drives to push himself out of whatever he was stuck in.

And that was going to take time.

At this point he had been working to get out for almost two years and maybe in another year he would reach the edge.

He almost thought about going back into cold sleep, but decided he needed to stay awake and pay attention for the years this would take.

Seemed like a good idea two boring years ago.

Not so much now.

He was working on some calculations and just happened to be sitting in his command chair in the three-person command center when things changed on the big screen in front of his chair.

There were thousands of small flashes of light along the surface of what seemed to be inside. And then, where a moment before it had shown a blank sort of nothingness, now the stars were back.

Lost Sense was back in regular space.

He jumped from his chair with both hands in the air and shouted "Yes!" Then he quickly went back to his instruments.

All his ship's systems were working.

Oh, wow, now he could have a good steak dinner, a glass of wine, and get back to sleep to complete his mission.

Only one big problem.

Nothing about space around him looked right.

Nothing at all.

At this point the small cluster galaxy should be filling space ahead of him, but there was nothing there.

The big spiral First Galaxy was farther away from him than he had lifetimes to return to, even if he was the oldest man alive.

None of this was possible.

None of it.

"Chairman Estrabrook?" a voice asked over his unused communications system.

Larry jerked. Looked around at the empty command center, then just sat back and laughed. He must still be in deep sleep and all of this was a malfunctioning sleep chamber causing him to dream. No one could be talking to him out here in literally the middle of nothingness.

"This is Chairman Evan West of the Seeder ship *Rescue Two*. Welcome back."

"Did I go somewhere?" Larry asked, wondering why this dream even had names in it.

At that point a ship so large it blocked out most of the stars on one side of his big screen flashed into existence and stopped.

He tried to get an image of the ship, but it was so large he failed.

He felt like a guppy next to a whale. He could tell that the new ship was in the shape of a bird of prey. He had heard rumors that the Seeders were going to design their ships like that, but it hadn't started when he left.

In two hundred years they had made a lot of progress, or something was really, really wrong.

"You were trapped in a Void Space Bubble," Chairman West said. "Time and space do not work the same inside of one of those, so we popped the bubble to get you out."

"Okay," Larry said, starting to feel a little panicked and starting to realize his mission was most likely over.

"With your permission, we would like to take your ship into our docking bay and get you to a Seeder Base. There are a lot of people who are excited to meet and talk with you."

"Why?" Larry asked.

"Because of how old you are," Chairman West said. "You have knowledge about the early days of the Seeders that has been long forgotten."

"How much time has passed?" Larry asked, not really wanting to know the answer, but it was starting to seem that if this was not a dream, he was going to have to face the answer.

"Just over seven million years," Chairman West said.

Again, Larry just laughed.

No way he could even begin to grasp seven million years.

But that explained the galaxies not being where they were supposed to be.

"And it was some of your friends who were also trapped in Void Space Bubbles that suggested we go looking for you."

"I have seven-million-year-old friends?" Larry asked.

"They were trapped for millions of years, just as you have been. Many of them always wondered what happened to you. So they told us, as best they could, what path you took and we found you."

"Thank you," Larry said.

He would have to ask later exactly what it took to find him and rescue him.

"Chairman Ray would like to talk with you for a few minutes," Chairman West said. "He is sort of the person who runs all the Seeders and has now for millions of years. Would that be all right? We'll bring you aboard and get your ship on our hanger deck. With your permission."

Larry just laughed. "Seems like I have no choice. Even at full speed, it would take me another million years to get back to the First Galaxy. How long will it take with you?"

"Five minutes," Chairman West said.

Larry once more laughed until he realized Chairman West was perfectly serious.

Larry took a deep breath and looked around. Nothing holding him here.

"Sure, I would be glad to talk with Chairman Ray and catch a ride home."

"Great," Chairman West said.

A moment later, with no feeling at all of movement, Larry found himself standing in an ultra-modern, yet surprisingly comfortable conference room with a long table and eight chairs, facing a man about Larry's height with a large smile on his face.

"It is an honor to meet you," Chairman West said, stepping forward and shaking Larry's hand.

"I think the honor is all mine," Larry said.

At that moment a man appeared next to Chairman West. He had long gray hair, perfectly straight that ran down his back, and wore slacks and a dress shirt that looked like it was right out of Larry's time.

Actually Chairman West wore about the same thing, so looked like fashions for Seeders hadn't changed much.

"I am Chairman Ray," the man said and stepped forward with his hand outstretched. "It is an honor to meet you, Chairman Estrabrook."

"Why is it an honor to meet me?" Larry asked. "You rescued me, from what I am starting to understand. This should be all my honor."

Chairman Ray smiled and nodded to West who brought up an image on the screen. It was of the First Galaxy and the surrounding smaller galaxies that orbited the First Galaxy.

"When you left on your mission," Ray said, "the First Galaxy was about half seeded with human planets."

Larry nodded to that.

"Where you were headed is now called The Misty Galaxy. When you were lost, your name became lore and a warning of the dangers of moving between galaxies in deep space. You were considered a hero."

"Well, I slept for two hundred years until I got stuck," Larry said. "I suppose that's heroic."

Chairman Ray ignored him and just went on. "Then a few thousand years after you were lost, one of the first of what we call Mother Seeder Ships with over four million souls on board, headed toward the Misty Galaxy. It also vanished without a trace into a different Void Space Bubble."

"We just found that ship last year," West said. "And it was many on board that ship that suggested we search for you. We will be taking you to the same base where most of them are at now."

Larry just nodded and said, "Thanks."

"Now let me show you what has happened since you have been gone," Ray said. "And what you started."

"All five of the satellite galaxies around the First Galaxy were seeded finally," West said.

The image on the screen pulled back to show all of them colored in a soft gold color.

"Then we moved out," Ray said, "and we ended up seeding almost one thousand galaxies at this point and are still expanding."

Larry again just laughed as the image pulled way back showing the orange points of light that represented full galaxies with billions and billions of stars in each one.

"There are millions and millions of human planets in each one of those lights," West said.

"A new Seeder Mother ship is now coming online every few weeks," Ray said, "and we are finishing the seeding of a new galaxy now about every three months."

Larry just moved over to a chair and sat down, shaking his head. He just felt tired and totally overwhelmed.

"We'll be docking in the *SunWorld Seeder Base* in a minute," West said.

"Where is my place in all of that now?" Larry asked, indicating the screen.

"Spend a few years learning what is happening now," Ray said, "see what is even possible, talk with some of your old friends, get used to being so far into your future."

"Is this possible to get used to?" Larry asked.

West laughed. "It is. And if you need help, we have it for you. Millions are going through what you are experiencing right now because once we discovered Void Space Bubbles and how to rescue those stuck inside them, we have been doing so regularly."

"And we hope you will spend some time with some of the Seeder historians," Ray said. "Help them fill in some holes in history."

Larry just laughed. "You mean my former world."

"Exactly," Ray said. "But isn't that the way it is for all of us as we age through all of our lives? Our worlds become former worlds. And those former worlds become history."

"Got that right," Larry said. "For some of us just a little quicker than others."

Both Ray and West had to agree to that.

SECTION ONE

THE FIRST SEARCH

CHAPTER 1

Chairman Evan West stood beside his command chair on the bridge of Seeder ship *Rescue Two*, letting the twenty-seven people on the three levels of stations in the command center work in silence around him. He knew that his crew of sixteen thousand were pretty much all as intensely focused as he was at this moment.

West was tall and thin and in great shape, standing just over six feet tall. He had green eyes and a smile that made others like him. And he loved to laugh and enjoy life, especially in this job.

His wife, Tammy Branch, had her dark hair pulled back tight away from her face as she almost always wore it while in the command center. She frowned at her screen one level above where he stood and to his right. He knew that tiny frown was not from a problem, but of extreme concentration.

He and Tammy made a perfect couple, always had. At

first, they had been on different ships, doing different missions for the Seeders. But after the mother ship she was on, *Dreaming Large,* had got trapped in a Void Space Bubble and it had taken him over sixteen years to lead *Rescue One* to free the mother ship, they had decided to be on the same missions.

And she had decided to help him with *Rescue Two.* And he needed her help more than anything.

And he loved that. They were both astrophysicists by training, and his study had led him to find the Void Space Bubbles and learn how to free ships from them. But since those few seconds she had been trapped that for him had been sixteen years, she had also focused all her attention on the Void Space Bubbles.

And he had to admit, she was now better with understanding and tracking them than he was. And he didn't mind that in the slightest. In fact, for *Rescue Two,* he depended on her.

Their apartment was large and comfortable, decorated in brown tones with lots of shelves of books, and they both had offices. And every day they made a point of eating dinner together at their glass kitchen dining table to talk over their days. Twice a week they had movie night on the big screen over the stone fireplace in their living room.

Popcorn and everything. He couldn't believe how much he looked forward to those nights.

That apartment had become their safe place, their place to go just relax away from the stress, stretch out and read a good book. It was their place and they did their best on normal days to leave the stress in the command center. But it turned out, some days on this mission didn't allow that.

Those sixteen years Tammy had been missing made West love her even more. Even though it had only been a few seconds for her actually being trapped, she seemed to understand and return the love and she was the one who had suggested the changes.

And wanted to help him in this crazy and important assignment.

After the war with the aliens had been won, primarily by his knowledge of Void Space Bubbles, Chairman Ray, the Seeder who seemed to guide all Seeders through thousands and thousands of galaxies, had given West an assignment.

Chairman West was to have his ship, *Rescue One,* refurbished and expanded, with the new fast speeds known to Seeders, and all modern equipment that had been developed during the war. He was to recruit a crew and then his mission was to find lost Seeder ships. More thousands of them than he wanted to actually think about that had gone missing over the centuries.

And he was to start, test *Rescue Two,* with two lost Seeder mother ships that had left the original Earth millions of years before and simply vanished.

Since mother ships could smash into a planet and come out the other side without damage, Ray and West both thought the ships had run into Void Space Bubbles, where time didn't really exist. If they were in Void Space Bubbles, the ships themselves might have only experienced a few weeks during those millions of years.

Rescue Two's job was to try, after all the millions of years, to track those ships and find them and rescue them, or find out what had happened to the millions of Seeders who had been on those two ships.

Each mother ship carried over a million in crew.

Ray had looked at West and said, "Some of my best friends were on those ships, Chairman. Find them. We need them more than ever right now."

West had only nodded.

It had taken three years to refurbish *Rescue One* into *Rescue Two*. And another two weeks to track where the first mother ship might have traveled in over eighty years of flight at the speeds of ships at that time.

Tammy's expertise as an astrophysicist was in space mapping through time, dealing with the galaxy shifts and drifts. Extremely high-level math that they had installed extreme levels of computers in *Rescue Two* just for her and her department.

And the movement of the Void Space Bubbles over time seemed to be even stranger.

He had heard Tammy once explain to someone that the Void Space Bubbles formed in the universe like bubbles in a carbonated drink, and her job was to track the exact location of the bubble after millions of years of the influences of the gravity from galaxies and black holes.

West just found it impressive, to say the least. He understood it at a basic level, but their entire mission depended on how well she could do that tracking.

Every night at dinner, since he understood her work, they

decided to talk about it for a set fifteen minutes to let off pressure, and he was damned proud of himself every time he could offer a suggestion that she actually took.

He had to admit, to someone listening in to one of their dinners from the outside, it would seem very strange, talking galaxy drift, gravitational influences, and Void Space Bubble formations.

"Dropping out of Trans Warp," James, his navigator said, "right on target."

West trusted James with just about anything, even though he looked like he had barely left college, with a baby face, blue eyes, and blond hair. Actually James was almost four hundred years old and maybe the top navigator to come out of the war.

If West and James hadn't been good friends back before the war, and hadn't worked a few ships together for Seeding, West would have never gotten such a great talent at the very place they needed him to be.

"Void Space Bubble should be right ahead of us," Tammy said.

"It is," James said.

"Take us to within scanning distance slow and carefully," West said.

Since the war, all Seeder ships could see clearly on their scans all areas of Void Space. But they were all still very careful around them, since one wrong move could cost them thousands of years lost until they either went through or got rescued.

This large bubble ahead of them had been on the assumed

flight path of one of the ancient Seeder Mother ships named *Dawn's Light*.

The Voice Space Bubble was as big around as about ten solar systems, one of the bigger ones West had dealt with. On his screens it almost looked alive, shimmering in extreme blackness. West knew that was his idea to make the bubbles actually look visible on the screen, even though they were not in real life. He just hated looking at a black screen. It made the bubbles feel even more dangerous, but adding the shimmering to their image took some of that feeling of danger away.

This particular bubble would have been on the edge of a galaxy at the time where the *Dawn's Light* would have been heading to possibly seed. Now the Void Space Bubble had shifted a great deal in space, but Tammy had tracked it through the five million years.

Actually, she had taken its position now, since they had spotted it, and backtracked it to where it would have been at the time of the flight of the mother ship. It was then that they realized it might be one they were looking for.

They all believed this one bubble was their best hope so far.

"Scanning distance," James said. "All stop."

Extreme silence in the command center.

Heavier silence than West could imagine being on this command center, which usually felt light and full of laughter and fun. It almost felt like the oxygen had been sucked out of the room.

One thing he liked about his crew, they knew when to enjoy their jobs and when to really focus.

This was focus time.

He made himself take slow, deep breaths.

After a moment, Tammy looked up at him from her screen, a smile on her face.

"Scans show a Seeder mother ship."

West pumped his fist into the air as around the command center applause and cheers filled the large room. West just stood there smiling, his hands in fists over his head in a victory sign.

Was this really going to be possible to do?

"Any idea with this size bubble how much time has passed for them?" James asked as the cheering died down and everyone went back into focus mode at their stations.

"Six days and a few hours," Tammy said. "For them."

West just shook his head. The massive ship, if it was the one they were hoping for, with over a million souls on board had been missing for over five million years.

"Let's set up to get them out of there," West said.

He hit his com link. "Ben, time to pop a big one."

"Copy that, Chairman," Ben said.

"Triple-check everything. Got a lot of people inside that thing."

"Will do," Ben said and signed off.

Ben was a short man who had once been military, but he and West had hit it off hundreds of years before and West could think of no one more suited to run the fifteen hundred small scout ships and all the support crews and pilots that manned the ships to plant the explosives in exact positions around the bubble.

The job of each ship would be to place explosives near the surface of the bubble in exact spots.

All explosives had to be blown at the exact same time to collapse the bubble without damaging anything inside. One wrong move and whatever was inside would be crushed, a move West and the Seeders fleet had used a lot during the war on trapped enemy ships.

West sat down in his command chair and said simply into a com link in the arm of his chair, "Chairman Ray."

Chairman Ray's stern face appeared almost instantly on the private screen directly in front of West's chair.

"We have a Seeder mother ship in a bubble," West said. "We think it is the *Dawn's Light*. I thought you might want to be here to greet them and help start them through the transition."

"How long until you have the bubble destroyed?"

"Thirty minutes," West said, glancing at the status report of all the small scout ships as they poured off the hanger decks of the *Rescue Two* and spread out around the bubble.

Ray nodded. "I will be right there in ten minutes."

West nodded and clicked off.

Then he stood and turned to his command center crew. "Stay sharp, people. Chairman Ray will be here shortly."

Then he smiled at Tammy, who smiled back before going back to work.

A good day.

At least so far.

CHAPTER 2

Chairman Ray appeared beside West's command chair and a slight gasp went out through the command center. West understood that feeling. Ray was the unofficial leader of all the Seeders and was well over five million years old. Seeders lived a very long time, but only some of the ancients were older and had lived as long as Ray.

And Ray had a presence about him with the dark slacks, silk white shirt, long gray hair combed perfectly down his back, and ramrod-straight posture.

Usually Ray had a perfect poker face and never seemed to get ruffled by anything, but at the moment his eyes were a little wide and he seemed to be biting his lip.

"Are you going to be all right?" West asked Ray, moving over closer to him so that his words would not be heard by any of his crew.

Ray nodded. "My brother is one of the chairmen on this

ship. For millions of years I have feared him lost forever, dealt with his death a long time ago. It was only with your discovery of Void Space Bubbles and the rescue of *Dreaming Large* and your wife that I had let myself hope again."

West just nodded. Not a thing he could say to that.

Not a thing.

West was only about twenty thousand years old. He couldn't imagine thinking that a loved relative had been lost for millions of years and now he had a chance to see them again.

Impossible to imagine.

They stood there in silence watching the shimmering black bubble on the screen and the dots indicating all the scout ships spreading around the bubble and into positions.

Silence, complete silence filled the command center. And damned if West could think of anything to say either.

So they just stood there.

"Chairman," James said, finally breaking the silence, "we are ready."

West glanced over at Tammy who nodded her agreement. As well as being an expert astrophysicist, she now knew more than he did about Void Space Bubbles. If she said they were ready, they were ready.

West stepped over and studied the read-outs on his command chair coming in from Ben and his vast array of ships and then nodded back to Tammy.

From what he could tell, they were ready.

"Are you ready, sir?" West asked, turning to Chairman Ray.

Ray nodded and said nothing.

"Ben," West said. "Get them out of there."

A moment later a few thousand small explosions showed the massive globe of the Void Space Bubble, then the next moment an ancient Seeder mother ship appeared.

In comparison to the modern, sleek Seeder ships, this one looked ancient in design, even though completely undamaged in any way.

"It is the *Dawn's Light,*" Tammy said, smiling.

The command center exploded in cheering and even a little crying.

West had to admit, he wanted to cry just a little as well, but he didn't.

"Please hail their chairman," Ray said.

"Coming on screen," James said.

On the big screen in front of them, a man who looked a great deal like Ray, only without the wear and the long gray hair, appeared standing next to a dark-skinned woman with a beaming smile.

"Hello, Cannon," Ray said. "Hello, Anna. This is Chairman Evan West of the *Rescue Two.*"

Ray introduced West, who managed, even with a huge smile, to say nothing and just bow his greetings slightly.

"Wow, what are you doing here?" Cannon asked. "And *Rescue Two?* I don't understand. And what are all the scout ships surrounding us?"

Someone on the *Dawn's Light* command center said something in the background. West had a hunch it was someone reporting that *Dawn's Light* was no longer anywhere where they were supposed to be.

And that a lot of time had passed.

Cannon and Anna both turned to listen for a moment.

Cannon then turned back to Ray and his face suddenly had a look of panic on it.

Anna looked the same.

"What happened, brother?"

"You were trapped for over six of your days in what is called a Void Space Bubble. Chairman West and his amazing crew found you and broke you out of that bubble."

"But how?" Anna asked.

"We need to talk in private first," Ray said. "Chairman West and his wife and I can meet you in your main meeting room?"

Cannon nodded and cut the connection and a moment later West found himself with Tammy standing beside Ray in a standard old-fashioned mother ship meeting room. A large wooden table ran down the middle, with ten comfortable cloth chairs around it.

Actually, in over five million years, the conference rooms hadn't changed enough to be of note. Just different material for the table.

Pictures of galaxies and plants covered the walls, just as they did in the *Rescue Two* meeting room.

West and Tammy stood back as Cannon and Anna came into the room to face Ray. All three embraced. For Cannon and Anna, it had been eighty-plus years since seeing Ray.

West had no idea how Ray was even holding it together for this meeting.

"How is Tacita?" Anna asked about Chairman Ray's wife.

"She is fine," Ray said, smiling. "She can join us later when you are ready."

Then all five of them sat after introductions had been made.

West found himself holding Tammy's hand under the table and she held his back just as tightly. He would ask her later how this felt for her.

"So tell us exactly what has happened," Cannon said. "And how did you and your modern-looking ship get here, let alone know we needed to be rescued."

Ray turned to West. "Chairman, would you like to tell my brother and his wife how you rescued your wife?"

He then turned back to his brother. "You will have questions, but hear him out completely first."

West nodded and went over the story of the *Dreaming Large* vanishing. And all the years it took to understand Void Space Bubbles and learn how to get ships out of them safely.

"So time does not work the same inside of these Void Space bubbles as outside," Anna asked after West was done. "Is that correct?"

All three of them nodded.

"My ship was missing for sixteen years," Tammy said. "To those of us inside, only a few seconds had passed."

"So how much time passes inside versus in real space?" Cannon asked.

"That depends on a lot of factors," Tammy said, "but mostly on the size of the Void Space Bubble."

"Was the bubble we were in large or small?"

"Large," Tammy said. "So the time difference was extreme."

"How long have we been missing?" Cannon asked, looking directly at Ray.

Ray just frowned. "Just over five million years."

Cannon sat back hard in his chair and Anna's eyes looked distant.

"You thought we were dead for over five million years?" Cannon asked softly.

"I did," Ray said.

CHAPTER 3

Silence, thick and very heavy filled the conference room.

West squeezed Tammy's hand, very glad she was beside him for this. Very, very glad.

Finally Ray asked if he may connect Cannon's ship with West's ship. "I have a presentation for you that I think will make you proud."

"Go ahead," Cannon said, looking at Anna who just was sitting shaking her head. West could not begin to understand what they were feeling right now. Impossible to grasp the passage of millions of years. The human mind, even Seeder minds, just can't.

"When you left on this mission eighty of your years ago," Ray said as a map of galaxies came up on the screen on the wall at the end of the table. "This was the number of galaxies we had seeded."

"Ten if memory serves," Cannon said, looking at the green dots in a tiny area of the wall screen.

Ray nodded. "Yes, ten. This is how many human galaxies now exist."

Ray changed the image of the map.

West was stunned at how massive the amount of green was, spreading like a plant over massive amounts of space. Every green dot an entire galaxy with billions of stars.

"Wow," Tammy said softly beside him. This kind of perspective was not something they always saw or paid attention to.

"We have so many mother ships," Ray said, "we are now seeding a new galaxy on the average of every ten days. And a new mother ship is coming online now almost every month."

"What is the gray area?" Anna asked after a moment of everyone staring at the incredible image.

"Those are the home galaxies of the Gray."

"The short little bald aliens?" Cannon asked.

Ray nodded. "They also live on every human seeded world as well and help us in the seeding process in a behind-the-scenes way. We have had a treaty with them since right after you vanished."

"And the black area," Cannon asked.

West looked down. Not something he wanted to talk about much.

"We had a war with a Seeder-made alien culture," Ray said. "Those are all dead galaxies."

"And the bright blue dot and line?" Anna asked.

"The Ancients' home world and the area we think they disappeared into," Ray said.

"Ancients?" Cannon asked.

West had no doubt this was going to take a lot of time to explain over many, many days.

"Yes, we were seeded as well," Ray said. "We call our Seeders the 'Ancients.'"

"Oh, shit," Anna said.

"We can ask Daniels to join us later," Ray said. "He can explain that part."

"Daniels?" Cannon asked, looking puzzled as to why Ray would want their second in command to join them.

"He's an Ancient," Ray said, "along with about eighty other crew members on this ship, riding along to help. I'm actually very interested in talking with them as well. Ancients are not enemies. They are Seeders as well. But all of them have just left their home worlds and no one knows exactly where they went."

"I am so confused," Anna said.

Tammy leaned forward. "Let me try to get you some grounding, since I was also trapped inside a Void Space Bubble and suddenly had six hundred ships surround us."

Anna nodded, as did Cannon.

"What happened is that without your knowing it, six days ago your time, you ran into a Void Space Bubble. Your engines shut down and nothing seemed to work as normal."

They both nodded.

"You could also no longer see real space, but you could see

the inside edge of the bubble and were trying to get to it with just your forward real-space motion, correct?"

Again they both nodded.

"For every second you existed in that bubble," Tammy said, "out here in standard time, years went past. And there was nothing at all you could do about it or change it. And there was nothing you did wrong at all. It has happened to many, many Seeder ships until my husband here and his team invented a way to scan for Void Space Bubbles and avoid them."

"We will be looking for the mother ship *Shadow Stars* next," West said. "It vanished about three hundred years after you did."

"It was Chairman Ray's desire to find you that got this mission going," Tammy said. "Although he did not tell us why exactly."

Cannon glanced at Anna, then back at Ray. "We need to tell our crew what happened. Can you give us some time?"

"Contact us when you need more answers," Ray said. "I have a fleet of ships headed this way that should start arriving at any moment, with the majority of them arriving tomorrow to help you retrofit your ship and get you into a Seeder port for a complete overhaul to get you and your crew five million years into the future."

"Any moment now?" Anna asked. "How fast are your ships?"

"We can make the journey that took you eighty years to make in a few hours at normal speeds. Faster if we had to."

Anna just sort of shook her head.

Cannon nodded and stood. "Thank you, brother," he said.

They hugged and then Ray nodded to Anna.

Then West, Tammy, and Ray were back in the command center of the *Rescue Two*.

West turned to his command crew and said simply, "Any question any of the crew of that ship have, no matter how stupid sounding, answer it carefully, fully, and with compassion."

Around the command center his crew was nodding.

West then turned back to Ray. Tammy had her arm around him and seemed to almost be holding him up.

Finally Ray seemed to gather himself and stand, his posture back completely.

"Thank you both for your amazing work on this," Ray said. "I need to tell Tacita that her brother-in-law and sister-in-law are very much alive and well. She was refusing to believe this possible. She and Anna were very close."

"We are here when you need us," West said.

Ray nodded. "I know that. But now I need you and your wonderful crew to see if you can find *Shadow Stars*. We will have this situation covered completely tomorrow with enough counselors to help a lot of those having issues with the time loss deal with it."

"We will start our search for *Shadow Stars* tomorrow then," West said.

And with that Chairman Ray nodded his thanks, smiled, and without a word vanished.

"Open a ship-wide com link," West said.

"Open."

"Well done, everyone, on finding and rescuing the million souls on *Dawn's Light.* We will be here for support duty for a very short time, more than likely not longer than a day, then we move on. So we celebrate tonight, then we start our search for *Shadow Stars*. There are a million souls on that ship that need our help. Well done, everyone."

He clicked off the com link and smiled at Tammy.

Everyone in the command center was smiling and chatting with someone else. It felt back to normal again, thankfully. Not sure how much of that intense focus time he could deal with.

"I suggest we have a nice dinner in our apartment, just the two of us," Tammy said.

He smiled and hugged her. "You know we have no hope of making more than an hour or so without getting called back here?"

"Then we better get going," she said, laughing. "You make the steaks, I'll do the salad."

"Deal," he said, and with that they vanished from the command center.

They actually got one hour and fifteen minutes before they were again needed. A wonderful one hour and fifteen minutes as far as West was concerned, because to him, he was really starting to understand the importance of time.

Both on a large scale and on a minute-by-minute level.

CHAPTER 4

Three long and frustrating weeks after finding *Dawn's Light,* West stood near his command chair in the command center, staring at the massive display screen in front of him. Around him the twenty-seven crew were silent, giving the three-level room a very unusual feel of tension.

He hated that feeling.

Usually this big, three-level room with the high ceilings was full of light chatter and sometimes laughter. And it seemed to always smell like freshly brewed coffee, since he allowed cups of coffee in the command center. Considering he and Tammy drank their fair share, it was only logical he should let his command crew do the same.

He actually liked the feel the coffee smell gave the command center. Less sterile-feeling. Tough to do since all the floors, walls, and workstations were an off-white plastic. But somehow the rich, lingering smell of coffee just softened everything.

What caused the unusual silence was that the massive wall screen in front of him showed a massive Void Space Bubble, by far the largest he had ever seen. Even the computer-added shimmering on the surface looked like it was forming waves it was so large.

In fact, they had to take down the magnification some just to get it to fit on the massive wall screen that filled the area in front of his command chair.

Actually, it was the largest bubble anyone had ever seen and reported.

Tammy said that theoretically, a bubble that large could not exist, but yet there it was.

This morning over breakfast, just after they found the bubble, West and Tammy had had a long discussion on how and why the gravitational forces of the universe and nearby galaxies had not torn the thing apart and destroyed whatever was inside of it, if anything.

The closest station to his chair on his right and up one level was where Tammy worked. She was shaking her head at the readings in front of her, never a good thing. She was the leading expert on Void Space Bubbles, how they were formed, how to tear them apart.

He was a close second, since he was the one that discovered them in the first place and rescued her from one, but in the years since she had gone by him in knowledge about them, and he admitted it.

She had her long brown hair pulled back tight, giving her

beautiful, classic face a hardness that actually went with the level and skill of her work.

And with what they were facing at the moment.

She was almost as tall as he was at six-two and in just as good of shape. They both worked out every day together.

The two of them made a powerful couple. Both were scary smart as someone had said, both had long brown hair they kept tied back, both loved their jobs beyond all reason.

Why wouldn't they love this job. They rescued people who were lost. What was not to love?

Rescue Two was a mid-sized Seeder's ship, shaped like a bird with wings back in a dive. West thought it beautiful. It had the state of the art Trans Warp drives that took them so fast that entire galaxies would flash past like fence posts along a country road at full speed.

It had a crew of sixteen thousand who all loved the idea of the ship's mission. And it carried over fifteen hundred other small scout ships that planted charges on the outside of the Void Space Bubbles to collapse them.

West wondered with a bubble this size did they have enough scout ships to safely pop the bubble.

Before they left on this journey, they had installed some of highest-level computers the Seeders knew, just for him and Tammy and for what she needed to do. Over two hundred of his crew were tasked with keeping those computers working and updating them 24/7.

Tammy was also the expert on board of tracing the locations of anything after millions of years of moving through space. Nothing in space ever stood still. It was all moving and often in different directions. That took massive computer power, more than he could even imagine.

And it took an astrophysicist's brain to even understand what was happening.

He glanced around at his command crew. All of them were dressed in their normal casual, just like he was. He spent every day in jeans, a comfortable long-sleeved shirt with the sleeves rolled up, and running shoes. He knew of no Seeder's ship that actually had uniforms of any kind.

Seeder ships were not military. They were all functioning businesses, which was why he was called Chairman. He ran the ship, basically owned the ship, and if the ship made money on its missions, the crew all made money.

So far, after finding and rescuing the lost Seeder mother ship *Dawn's Light*, this mission was far, far into profit.

At the moment over half his command crew were working on something at their stations, the few remaining were doing as he was doing and staring at the representation of the massive Void Space Bubble.

"How large is that thing?" he asked, giving Tammy enough time to actually get measurements.

"Over a half-a-light-year in diameter," Tammy said.

He could not even imagine something that size as one unit.

"Could *Shadow Stars* be in there?" he asked.

The *Shadow Stars*, a Seeder mother ship with over a million on board, had vanished just at five million years ago. And the theory was that it had run into a Void Space Bubble and got stuck where a week or two ship time might have gone by for them, but millions of years would have passed outside the bubble.

Right now, *Rescue Two's* entire mission was to find that Void Space Bubble *Shadow Stars* was in and free it.

It seemed the larger the bubble, the greater the difference between the time inside and the time flowing past outside. Tammy had tried to explain the math of that to him one night over a bottle of wine. Not much of the explanation stuck for some reason, even with his training.

"*Shadow Stars* is not in this one," Tammy said. "Over the last five million years, this bubble has moved to this location from a sector of space we have not explored at all. Even to this day."

"Let's see if it has caught anything," West said. "Move us to scanning distance carefully."

"Yes, sir," James, his pilot and good friend said from his left.

Even though all Seeder ships could see the exact boundary of every bubble, the practice was to stay back from the edge like a hiker would from a crumbling cliff and then scan.

"We need to get rid of this one," Tammy said, turning to him. "No matter what we find inside. Too large to let it continue to grow. I am still puzzled as to how it got this big, to be honest."

West nodded. He was just as puzzled as she was.

"Ben," West said, "prepare to launch enough ships to take this monster out."

"Going to be close," Ben's response came back. "I'll double

up on a number of the ship's explosives, so going to take some time to set everything."

"Let me know when ready," West said. "No hurry."

Tammy nodded and turned back to her board. West knew Ben would have the scout ships fanning out around the bubble and standing by.

If they didn't set off detonations to pop the bubble at exactly the same time , whatever was inside would be crushed.

"Scanning distance," James said. "All stop."

"Scans started," Cynthia said from directly behind him. She was in charge of all scans of Void Space Bubbles. She was married and had two kids onboard and her husband was one of the lead scout pilots who set the explosives. She might be the shortest human on the entire ship at four-foot-three. But wow was she powerful.

Silence filled the command center as everyone waited.

At least until Cynthia said, "Oh, shit."

That was the first time West had ever heard her swear.

CHAPTER 5

West looked back at the pale face of Cynthia. Normally she had a lot of reds and pinks in her skin, but something inside the bubble had caused her to be almost in shock.

"On the big screen," West said.

She nodded and he turned around as the scan of the interior of monster bubble came up. It took him a moment to understand what he was seeing.

One massive ship, and maybe at least two thousand smaller ships. The massive ship looked to be about the size of a Seeder mother ship.

And every ship was alien.

Clearly alien.

Seeder ships all looked like birds in flight with wings folded back. This huge ship looked more like a super fat rocket with giant fins.

Now Seeders, when they scouted a new galaxy to seed, avoided any alien civilization of any kind that was trying to develop. The Seeders just avoided that galaxy and moved on to the next galaxy to seed. Advanced life of any kind was very, very rare, it seemed.

Avoiding all aliens, advanced or in the early stages of development, was a hard and fast rule of all Seeders.

Only the Gray and humans (which the Seeders were a subset of) actually had gotten out of their own systems and then out of their own galaxy.

West knew that a number of alien cultures had managed to get out of their own home systems, but there were none in all the millions of galaxies that had been scouted besides the Gray that had gone beyond that.

Seeders had a long-standing agreement with the Gray and when a new world and galaxy was seeded, Grays always helped and took up residences on the new planets in the desert areas.

How this fleet of alien ships had gotten trapped in this massive bubble meant they had to have at least been between systems in their galaxy in some form or another, but more than likely between galaxies. Void Space Bubbles didn't tend to form inside galaxies. They got torn apart by the gravity too easily. They needed the openness of space between galaxies.

"All right, people," West said. "I need data and I need it now."

Everyone broke from staring at the fleet on the screen and went back to work with a sudden wash of sound through the command center.

"Tammy," he said. "Any idea how long they have been in there?"

"Working on that," Tammy said, her head down, her face covered with an intense frown.

"I'm going to get help on the way," West said and moved over and sat down in his command chair. Then he contacted Chairman Ray, who for the last five plus million years had been the unofficial leader of the Seeders.

It took a moment, but then Chairman Ray's face appeared. "Chairman West, any luck finding *Shadow Stars?"*

Chairman Ray had a square face, seldom smiled. West liked the man, but could not imagine living that long.

"Not yet," West said. "But we are on their trail. But we did run into something that is going to require help. More than likely a lot of help. We have found a Void Space Bubble larger than anything we have ever seen before by about double."

Ray nodded and West went on.

"Inside it is an entire alien fleet of some sort."

West sent him the image of the fleet inside the bubble.

West watched as Chairman Ray's eyes grew round.

"What have you learned about this feet of ships?" Ray asked.

"Just discovered it," West said.

"The fleet has been trapped in the bubble for almost eight million years," Tammy said. "About a week in their shipboard time frame."

West shook his head and Chairman Ray looked off to his right for a minute. Then he turned back.

"They are not in our data base of known alien civilizations.

But they were trapped in there before we even broke out of our own galaxy and started seeding."

"Would the Ancients or the Grays maybe know who they are?" West asked.

"They might," Ray said, nodding. "In the meantime I'll have a mother ship headed your way with a couple hundred science vessels as well. They will be at your position tomorrow early."

"Thank you, sir," West said. "We'll keep running scans."

Ray nodded and his image vanished.

"The Ancients won't know them," Tammy said. "This bubble in eight million years has drifted in from an area of the universe we have never gotten around to sending any ships into, from a distance so great that before the upgrade of our ships to the faster speeds, we could have never imagined."

"So what in the hell are we going to do with them?" West asked, looking back up at the huge fleet stuck in time and space in front of him.

"Give them a nearby galaxy, since we haven't started seeding it yet," Tammy said, shrugging. "And then run like hell."

West nodded. Not a bad idea at all.

The running part.

CHAPTER 6

By the time he and Tammy staggered back to their large apartment to try to get some sleep, they had discovered a lot more about the alien race in front of them.

They were a form of humanoid, looking like a cross between the Gray and a human. Hairless, short, but with eight fingers on each hand and eight toes on each foot and they seemed to be able to use all thirty-two digits at the same time for different tasks. They also seemed to have three sexes.

They lived about the same lifespan as humans, not the long lives of Seeders.

The aliens were military at the core, but their weapons were pretty basic and all the smaller ships were not military ships, but more transport ships with small crews. Basically all those smaller ships carried the supplies for the millions living on the big ship.

Everything was designed on that fleet for a long journey and it wasn't until right before West and Tammy were to head off to bed that they discovered none of the ships had a faster-than-light drive.

This was a generation fleet that had, for some reason, left its own system to travel to another system and this Void Space Bubble had grabbed them early on, more than likely near the edge of their galaxy.

The aliens had planned the trip to take over two hundred years in human time.

That just impressed West more than he wanted to admit. The *Rescue Two* would take a fraction of a second at very slow speed to cross the distance that fleet had planned to take two hundred years.

Humanity had never had to try that sort of thing. Humanity developed the first basic Trans Warp drive and every planet they seeded, every Earth, developed it about the same time.

Early humanity took weeks to get between systems inside a galaxy, but compared to two hundred years, that was a blink.

So the next morning, they had given Chairman Ray all their findings and he said he would be there in ten minutes. Seeders can also teleport and someone like Ray can teleport over massive distances.

West could teleport across the width of a galaxy, but he would never try the distances Ray seemed to do without thinking about them.

Ray appeared exactly ten minutes later next to West's command chair.

West and Tammy were standing there, waiting for him.

Chairman Ray nodded to both of them. "So these poor people got stuck in this bubble eight million years ago in a galaxy so far from here, we haven't even thought about going out there? Could you figure out what their origin galaxy even was?"

Tammy nodded. "It was a satellite cluster-shaped galaxy that orbited around a large spiral. It was consumed by the spiral about four million years ago and now no longer exists."

Chairman Ray nodded.

"Any ideas?"

West glanced at Tammy and she nodded that he should go ahead.

"We free them and destroy that monster bubble in the process," West said. "There is an Earth-like planet near this location just inside that spiral galaxy, orbiting a yellow star. It has the kind of environment they need to survive and thrive. We have not even scouted this galaxy yet."

Chairman Ray nodded. "Our policy is to never connect with a lower-level alien culture."

"I know," West said and went on. "One of our mother ships should be able to tow that big alien ship and all of the fleet in tractor beams at the same time to the planet and put it in a stable orbit. Their weapons are harmless against our ships."

"Without telling them what we are doing or communicating with them at all?" Chairman Ray asked.

"As long as we have enough ships to make them look impossibly outnumbered," West said. "We could figure out how to say in their language that we come in peace, take a day to tow them to their new home and vanish back into the stars, leaving a ship hidden to watch them."

Chairman Ray nodded. "That will work, but I want all the data confirmed before we release them. The *Golden Orb* will be here in a few hours, along with about eighty science ships. And the *Golden Orb* holds thousands of fighters as well."

"You won't need any of that," Tammy said. "These folks are babies compared to us."

"Just for show," Chairman Ray said, smiling. "Would you make sure the giant bubble gets destroyed safely, then leave the rest to the *Golden Orb* to deal with our lost alien friends, and get back on your mission to find *Shadow Stars.*

"Sounds like a perfect idea," West said. "We'll have the aliens out of there an hour after the *Golden Orb* shows up. Then be on our way."

"Thank you," Chairman Ray said. "And this was an amazing find. Going to be very interesting to see how our very short interaction with this race develops over time."

"That it will be," West said, smiling.

A moment later Chairman Ray vanished.

And about half the command crew jumped to get a fresh cup of coffee in relief of him being gone.

For the moment things were back to normal.

CHAPTER 7

The giant Void Space Bubble turned out to be a little more difficult to destroy safely than planned. And it took every scout ship they had to get enough explosives in positions to blow it. That took two extra hours to set up everything, instead of only the planned one hour after the mother ship arrived.

And they checked it three times because if they got something wrong, the collapse of the Void Space Bubble would smash the entire fleet and kill all the millions onboard the alien ships.

Finally both Tammy and West were satisfied and West gave the order and the alien fleet just sort of appeared.

The linguistics people on the *Golden Orb* managed to figure out enough of the alien language from tapping the alien computers once the bubble was gone to create a message.

"We come in peace to help."

As West and Tammy watched and all the scout ships were loaded back on board, the *Golden Orb* moved in close to the alien ship and then somehow got connected to it with massive tractor beams and started to pull it and all the smaller ships as a unit toward the designated system nearby.

West knew that they had to be very careful that they didn't tear apart the big alien ship, and it looked like that was working as well. And the towing speed was about a hundred times faster than the alien fleet could travel on their own. But still going to take a few days.

The *Golden Orb* just kept repeating over and over that they came in peace to help.

"Okay, folks," West said as they all watched for a good half hour and it looked like the alien fleet would be in position in a few days around their new home. "Great job with this. Now we still have a Seeder mother ship to find and rescue. Get us back on course and on mission."

There was laughter and some talking as his fantastic crew worked, then suddenly the *Golden Orb* towing the big alien ship and all its smaller ships vanished.

"Back on course, sir," James said. "Two hours to the next Void Space Bubble."

"Call me when you get close," West said. "Tammy I will be having lunch."

"Understood," Chairman," James said.

West and Tammy teleported to their apartment and both went to work putting together a salad and sandwiches. Their place,full of brown tones, a ton of bookshelves, and soft carpet in the living room and the bedrooms, always made West relax, even for a short lunch.

"That sure felt good," Tammy said after a few minutes.

West only laughed. "Saving millions of lives at a time, alien or human, never gets dull."

"So true," she said, and kissed him before going back to working on the sandwiches.

"Any chance *Shadow Stars* will be in this upcoming bubble?" he asked as he put the salad on their dining-room table and went to get silverware and dressing.

"None," she said. "We're still too far away from their reported track when they vanished."

"But no telling what will be inside this next one," he said. "Right?"

"And that's the fun of all this," she said, laughing. "Like opening a present from the distant past every time we pop a bubble."

He could not disagree in any way.

CHAPTER 8

West sat in his chair in the command center.

He had to admit, he seldom sat in the comfortable leather chair except for communications off ship, preferring to stand most of the time, but at the moment he was just waiting for Tammy to finish her calculations and put her findings on the big screen so all seventeen of the command crew could see what was happening.

Tammy had her long hair pulled back out of her face and wore her normal jeans, nice blouse, and running shoes. Both of them had been married before they met each other, but both of their previous marriages had just faded off with the passing of hundreds of years. He sure hoped he and Tammy didn't end up that way.

So far working together on this crazy rescue mission was making them closer. A lot closer. To him, it felt like he was falling deeper in love with her every day.

The silence in the big room was unusual as everyone waited. The center had enough stations to hold upwards of fifty people, but seventeen was all he ever needed at a time.

All stations faced basically forward, which was the wall-sized screen in front of him. Sometimes that screen showed the space around them, other times it would show data.

That design was standard Seeder command center design and he thought it stupid, to have everyone working for him behind him. But so far he hadn't come up with anything better.

And like normal, right now the room had a deep, rich smell of coffee. West bet at this point, the walls themselves in here smelled like coffee.

West, for a while, had thought their mission to find the *Shadow Stars* would be easy because right after they started they had found the *Dawn's Light*. That took only a few weeks and had been the first half of their mission.

Turns out he was wrong about the ease of things and the why he was wrong was what Tammy was going to try to explain in just a few minutes. She had tried it yesterday over dinner to him, but after a bit he had decided she needed to do it for the entire command crew.

And also, he hoped, give them a plan on where to search next.

"I'm ready," Tammy finally said, glancing back at him and he nodded.

She put up on the screen a two-dimensional image of human seeded space five million years ago. Only ten galaxies were seeded at that point. A green line led from one galaxy past a few others to a point that blinked.

The *Shadow Stars* mother ship had been on the way to seed a galaxy that was close to where they vanished.

West knew the *Shadow Stars* had taken almost a hundred and fifty years to travel that distance. *Rescue Two* could make the same trip in hours now.

"The green line," Tammy said, "is the path *Shadow Stars* traveled before it vanished. This is an image of how space looked five million years ago in their time."

West nodded when she glanced and him, so she went on.

"Now, if we add normal galactic movement over the five million years to get this to present time, this is what it would look like."

The image moved and seemed to swirl. In the bottom of the screen a counter clicked off over the millions of years. The line that *Shadow Stars* had traveled moved, bent, and even broke in places, entire galaxies merged and others came into the area. The blinking green dot showing *Shadow Stars'* reported last position moved as well.

Because *Shadow Stars* had vanished, the movement of the seeding ships five million years before had gone in another direction, so none of the galaxies around them had been seeded, but most had been recently scouted, so West knew that *Shadow Stars* had not ended up in any of them.

The movement of space and galaxies certainly wasn't like a straight-forward river. It looked more like an eddy beside a river, swirling, some lines moving faster than others, other areas seemingly going against the current.

It took massive computers for Tammy to even begin to calculate all this over those five million years. And it took him discovering how to see Void Space Bubbles in his search for Tammy when she was trapped in one that even made this search possible after all the years that had passed.

"We are now basically sitting here with normal galactic drift where the *Shadow Stars* would be," Tammy said, "right where the blinking light is. But no ship."

West nodded to that.

"So the question is, if *Shadow Stars* is in a Void Space Bubble, as we are assuming it is because of how it suddenly vanished, where did that Void Space Bubble go?"

CHAPTER 9

Silence filled the command center waiting for Tammy to answer her own question.

"There is some evidence that Void Space Bubbles," Tammy said, "don't travel at the same speed as the galactic movement around them."

West nodded. He knew that and also knew that area of study was now being studied in a dozen programs in Seeder bases. He and Tammy were getting findings from them all the time and Tammy was about to use some of those findings in this presentation.

"And there is a chance that *Shadow Stars* moved farther along its intended course before being trapped," Tammy said. "Let me take that possibility first."

She reset the big screen to the original image of only ten seeded galaxies and the straight-line course of the *Shadow Stars,* then added a short blinking green line to the end of it.

"They would have had to travel another year to cover that distance before vanishing," she said. "Sometimes they did not report back for a year's time."

She set that in motion with the counter again showing the speed of five million years in galactic time passing.

The end of the blinking green line moved almost in a completely different direction.

"That movement is caused by being caught up in the gravitational pull of a couple passing galaxies," Tammy said.

"Scan that area?" West said, standing up.

"Already have," Tammy said. "I have five different Void Space Bubbles in that general area. And six more between here and there.

All those bubbles appeared as marked red dots on the screen.

"But there are other alternatives," she said. "Using those two main areas, the one we are at now and the projected one if they had gone farther than reported."

He nodded and sat back down.

"If a large bubble just fractionally moved slower," Tammy said, "from this location, over five million years it would not be here, but in this position."

Seven more red dots appeared to one side of their location. And then eight more red dots appeared to the same side of the blinking green line.

"And if it moved faster," Tammy said, "it would be in this area."

Again on the big screen over a dozen red dots appeared to

the other side of their location and then eight more appeared near the end of the blinking line.

"There are other possibilities," Tammy said, "but these have the highest probability of success."

Silence filled the command center as West sat and stared at all the red dots on the map. No wonder the Seeders had lost so many ships. Those bubbles seemed to be everywhere.

He knew they could scan a Void Space Bubble and then destroy it in the space of two hours. So in a day they could do four or five of those red dots. So they would have their answer in a fairly short time considering.

"Let's assume they reported their last position at the time fairly accurately," West said, standing up. "So Tammy, is it more likely a large bubble would move slower than the space around it or faster. Any probability at all difference."

"Slower," she said, smiling. On the screen the slower moving bubbles were highlighted.

"So we go that way first," he said, smiling back at her.

He turned to James who was also smiling. "Set a course. Let's get these bubbles popped."

CHAPTER 10

During the rest of that day they scanned and then destroyed four empty Void Space Bubbles.

On the fifth one they found a Seeder search ship named *Sky Origin*.

"That's the search ship that traveled for over a hundred years to search for *Shadow Stars* just to vanish as well," Tammy said. "The fact that a mother ship and then a search ship both vanished is why the seeding went in a different direction."

"How many on board?" West asked.

"There are over six hundred people on that ship," Tammy said. "Chairman's name is Beverly DeSoto."

An image of DeSoto appeared on the big screen along with the image of the ship, clearly an old-style Seeder exploration ship. Same sweep-back wing design, just with more edges and crudeness to it.

"How long have they been in there, ship time?" West asked.

"Just over a month," Tammy said. "They would have worked their way out in another month ship time."

"Get them out of there," West said.

It took over two hours, as normal, to set all the charges to pop the bubble and not destroy the ship inside. Almost a thousand charges all had to go off at the same time to deflate the bubble, all placed perfectly around the edges. No problem. Ben and his people were very good at what they did, of that there was no doubt.

When the charges went off, and *Sky Origin* appeared in real space, West said, "Connect me to their chairman."

A moment later Beverly DeSoto appeared. She had long blond hair, bright green eyes like West's eyes, almost pink skin, and a panicked look on her face.

"Chairman Evan West," he said, "of the Seeder ship *Rescue Two*. Welcome back, Chairman Desoto. Would it be possible for my wife and I to talk with you and some of your top crew to explain what happened to you?"

She nodded, then glanced around for a moment, then turned back, her eyes wide. "My crew says millions of years have passed. Is that accurate?"

"It is," West said. "We can explain why."

"And we also are in search of the *Shadow Stars*," Tammy said, "and your knowledge might be amazingly helpful."

Chairman DeSoto nodded.

West and Tammy went onboard the ship, and with Chairman DeSoto's permission, and talked to the eight members of the command center. Before he went on board, West reported to Chairman Ray what they had found and Ray had told him that a mother ship with everything needed to help all the people on board would be at their location in ten hours.

Three of the command crew and Desoto agreed to help supply the data they had on *Shadow Stars* and were not only stunned that so much time had passed, but that a ship would be there to help them in just hours over the same distance that had taken them over a hundred years.

The next morning, when the massive mother ship *Nebula Blue* suddenly appeared out of Trans Warp, Tammy was excited. She had spent most of the night plugging in the new data from *Sky Origin* and it seemed even if they had searched all fifty of those bubbles that she had found, they still would have missed *Shadow Stars*.

West tried to get some sleep, but with Tammy working and so excited, he mostly stayed up to help her.

And then cook her breakfast.

That morning in the command center, she had the big map up on the screen. Chairman Desoto, eyes red, but seemingly fine, stood beside West, staring at the big screen.

Also both chairmen of the *Nebula Blue* stood beside her. Pat Geddes and Ruth Hoseley. Both almost looked like brother and sister, even though West knew they were married. They were both short, dark-skinned with long, straight dark hair pulled back. They were amazingly friendly and West liked them at once.

And Chairman Ray joined them at the last moment, his

intenseness and long gray hair down his back put West's crew on edge. But when he appeared he greeted Chairman DeSoto as an old friend and then shared a laugh with the chairmen of the *Nebula Blue*.

"It seems," Tammy said, starting her presentation, "that the data about the path of *Shadow Stars* didn't survive so well down through the millions of years. We were actually following the path taken by *Sky Origin* because it was much closer documented than a mother ship's path. Great reporting," Tammy said to Chairman DeSoto who bowed slightly in thanks. To her, that reporting had been going on regularly just recently.

Silence in the big command center as everyone sort of took in that information.

"I have blinking on the screen in blue the path of *Sky Origin*, which we thought was *Shadow Stars*. Here is the actual path of *Shadow Stars* from the records of *Sky Origin*."

The line stopped short of the original end point they had been following.

"Now I put the image into motion taking into account the five million years of movement of the galaxies."

Again the lines moved and shifted as the counter at the bottom of the screen went through the five million years in about ten seconds.

The end of the line was closer to the original departure galaxy than they had all thought.

Chairman DeSoto nodded. "When we found no trace of the ship in that area, we moved on figuring that they had gone farther than they had reported."

"We were starting to think the same thing," West said.

"The *Shadow Star* should be trapped in this exact Void Space Bubble," Tammy said. "Only one in that entire area that could hold them."

West smiled at his wonderful wife, then looked around. "Anyone interested in taking a little jump to see if the big ship is there?"

"Try to stop us," DeSoto said. "But since we are so slow, can we catch a ride?"

The chairman of *Nebula Blue* said of course and as soon as *Sky Origin* was loaded up into one of the mother ship's massive flight bays, they jumped to the Void Space Bubble.

Shadow Star was there.

And five million years after it started, Chairman DeSoto got to accomplish her mission of finding the lost mother ship.

Four hours later, *Rescue Two* had the big ship released from the bubble and ships of all kinds started pouring in to help the millions onboard who had just lost five million years in just over three weeks in a large bubble.

Four days later Tammy and West talked with Chairman Ray and suggested that they use old records of vanished ships and see how many they could find. In other words, do it as their long-term mission.

A new mission.

Ray just smiled and said, "I hoped you would think that. I have a list."

Tammy looked up at Ray and asked, "How many are on this list?"

"Put it this way. The list covers over seven million years," he said, smiling.

"Perfect," West said, hugging Tammy. "Because it never gets old rescuing people."

Tammy agreed and kissed him.

"Good," Chairman Ray said. "Because it never gets old being there when you two rescue them."

SECTION TWO

THE GALACTIC MISSING

CHAPTER 11

West watched the blank image on the big screen that filled one wall of the command center.

Around him, the seventeen command crew stood watching in silence, the air seeming to not even move as they also watched the screen intently, just waiting.

West and the crew were all waiting for Tammy to see if her calculations made it possible to go after the oldest missing ship in Seeder records.

It seemed that almost on every mission, he and the command crew waited breathlessly for Tammy to give them an answer on something. He wasn't certain he would ever get used to that.

The oldest missing Seeders ship had been missing outside the original galaxy for humans for just over seven million years. It was one of the first Seeder ships with the intent of planting humanity in other galaxies.

It had been slow going for the next two million years in getting humanity spread out after that ship vanished, but Seeders had managed to fill the original ten galaxies with humans in those two million years. But ships had continuously gone missing in the space between galaxies. And no one really knew why which meant that millions of years of missing ships were out there, more than likely just stuck in time.

That was the new mission for *Seeders Two*. Find all the trapped ships and release them.

And West and the crew had no doubt that mission would take not only years, but maybe decades.

Ray had given them a list of the known missing ships.

A massive list that numbered just over two million missing ships and who knew how many crew.

West could not believe that number. Two million.

West had just laughed when he got that total.

Tammy had had to sit down because while he looked at the number of ships, she automatically went to the people inside of all of the ships.

Chairman Ray said he would set up entire mother ships to carry counselors and other professional help for the ships they found. And so far there were entire Seeder bases set up for the found crews.

Most of those crews from the ships *Rescue Two* had already found did great moving up in time. But a few had real problems with it, and a few hundred were actually in hospitals.

One of the many problems was with the older missing ships the records of when they went missing was sometimes sketchy. Also, for the really old ones, the movement of the galaxies and the Void Space Bubbles themselves had to be calculated. Over millions of years it was stunning to West how much space itself changed.

And that was Tammy's job. She had the programs in their massive computers to calculate the movements and drifts of the galaxies. And now, since they were starting from near the original ten seeded galaxies, the oldest civilizations, they had decided to try to find the most famous of all missing ships, the *Sky Fall* mother ship, the second mother ship meant to seed galaxies ever built. It had four and a half million people on board and was commanded by Chairman Ben Carnay and his wife Risa Reeth.

After it went missing, the population of the mother ships had gone down to just over a million. Losing *Sky Fall* just cost them too many Seeders.

Chairman Ray, who had lived for over five million years and had come out of First Galaxy, said the loss of *Sky Fall* was before his time.

For seven million years, the mention of *Sky Fall* had been used to illustrate how dangerous open space could be.

Back when *Sky Fall* left the First Galaxy, to get to one of the First Galaxy satellite galaxies, it would have taken *Sky Fall* almost four hundred years. It would take *Rescue Two* now less than a minute.

West had warned Chairman Ray that if they did find *Sky Fall* stuck in a bubble, after seven million years, getting those four million people acclimated to this new world would be very, very difficult, if not impossible for many of them.

Chairman Ray had agreed and had said he would get the preparations started just in case they did find the ship.

Both West and Tammy were pretty sure they would find it.

So now, two weeks later, the *Rescue Two* second mission had officially started and West and the entire command crew were all waiting for Tammy to decide if they could find *Sky Fall* as their first ship of the new mission or not.

Finally, she stood and smiled at him, that wonderful smile he loved so much lit up her eyes and she let out a deep breath.

"Found it!" she said, smiling. "And chances are numbers of other ships as well."

CHAPTER 12

Tammy, smiling wider than West had seen his wife smile in a long time, pointed to the big screen in front of West's command chair and an image of the spiral First Galaxy came up, also showing the other nine satellite galaxies around it that comprised the first ten seeded galaxies.

"*Sky Fall* was headed between the First Galaxy and what is now called Misty Cluster," Tammy said, focusing in on those two galaxies on her two-dimensional map on the screen. "The ship vanished halfway. So I assumed a large Void Space Bubble was there."

She marked it with a bright red dot.

"Now to show the movement of the galaxies and the Void Space Bubble over seven million years of time."

West was surprised that the First Galaxy and the satellite galaxies around it just circled and moved closer or father away from each other, but overall in seven million years stayed amazingly stable.

However, the red dot did not. It moved from its original position and seemingly out into the void farther from the First Galaxy.

"That is directly on a line toward where many early Seeder ships traveled," she said. "In fact, over the millions of years, we have records of almost a dozen ships vanishing where this bubble traveled."

"Oh, my," West said. "James, take us to the bubble and stop within scanning distance."

"Three minutes" he said.

Longest three minutes West could remember living.

Halfway through he turned to Tammy. "Could you put up the list of missing ships you think might be in there, what years they went missing, and what size and type?"

She nodded and the image on the screen was replaced by a list of thirty-one ships, ranging from a fairly recent scout ship with a crew of eight thousand that had vanished three hundred years ago, to the *Sky Fall* mother ship with over four million on board and had vanished seven million years ago.

West could only shake his head at the idea that all of them could be in that one stupid Void Space Bubble.

"All stop," James said. "Scanning now."

"It's a huge bubble," Tammy said, "so the time inside it will be very, very slow if they are in there. The three hundred years of the scout ship will only be about five minutes to them."

After a moment Tammy said, "Oh, shit," and looked up at

West as everyone in the command center stopped and stared at her. She had a haunted look in her eyes that he had never seen before.

"They are all in there. The *Sky Fall* and all the rest on our list, plus a few not on our list, and four Gray ships as well."

The command crew broke out into cheering.

West allowed himself a little happy dance, then went up and kissed his smiling wife, then went and sat down in his command chair and connected to Chairman Ray with one simple message. "We have found *Sky Fall*. Come quick."

As West stood, Chairman Ray appeared at his side.

Around them the command crew were still applauding and laughing and talking.

"See that list on the screen?" West said to the unofficial leader of the Seeders. "They are all in there, plus two others we haven't identified yet, plus four Gray ships."

"Five Gray," Tammy said without looking up from her scanning.

"Five," West said, smiling at the shocked face of Chairman Ray. Hard to shock a man who had lived for over five million years. But they just had.

He just stood there staring at the names on the screen for a moment before he turned to Tammy. "Can you tell how much time has passed onboard the *Sky Fall*?"

"Twenty-one days," she said. "They were trapped on year one hundred and twelve of their mission."

"Same chairman in charge?" Ray asked.

"As far as I can tell," Tammy said. "Time in there is moving so slowly, to me, everyone in there is frozen in an instant of time."

Ray nodded, then turned to West. "Great work." Then he turned to Tammy. "To both of you and to everyone here."

He turned and bowed slightly to the command crew, who all bowed back.

Then Ray turned back to West. "Keep scanning and see if you can get me a final list of all the ships in there. I have to talk with the Gray first and that will take some time. Then I will get a massive fleet of ships headed here to help with this when we release them all at once."

"Yeah," West said, shaking his head and smiling. "We're going to need help with this one for sure. But you told us to find lost ships."

Chairman Ray just laughed. "I did, didn't I?"

Then he vanished.

CHAPTER 13

It took almost two weeks to get everything set up. For most of that, West and Tammy and the *Rescue Two* crew just kept doing research on the ships inside, what the name of each ship's Chairman was, and anything special about the crew or the contents.

And of course, since they were experts in safely destroying Void Space Bubbles without destroying the ships inside, it would be up to West and Ben and his crew to do the rescue.

Tammy told West one night over dinner that the two weeks that had passed while Chairman Ray got things set up would be less than a second to everyone inside the bubble.

Almost all the ships that waited back from the bubble were actually crew ships that could hold many, many thousands of crew and families each in comfortable apartments.

And except for *Sky Fall*, the ships the Gray had sent could hold other ships on their flight decks. *Sky Fall* would have to be updated right where it sat, at least the engines.

Even the most recent ship trapped by the bubble, the scout ship, was outdated and surprisingly slow. Seeders had made vast strides forward in just the last few centuries, after making almost no progress in millions of years.

Of course there were thousands and thousands of specialists to help with the reaction of losing so much time. After West and *Rescue Two* had found the first two mother ships that were missing, the counselors and specialists were getting better and better. Just not a job anyone needed before, helping people through traveling millions of years into their own future.

West knew they were getting close to the go time when a dozen Gray ships appeared out of Trans Warp. That was actually the first time West had seen the pencil-thin Gray ships with their black finish. Even stopped, they looked like they were moving.

At first there had been some talk about broadcasting to every Seeder ship what had happened, explain it all at the same time, but the situation of every ship was so different, that was decided against.

So each rescue ship was assigned a lost ship to contact.

Chairman Ray, West and Tammy, and Chairman Geddes and Hoseley of the mother ship *Nebula Blue* would be in charge of getting all the people off the *Sky Fall* and would greet and talk with the Chairman of *Sky Fall*.

So finally everyone was ready to go. They were about to

embark on the largest rescue mission in the millions of years of the Seeders history.

West and Ben and his entire fleet of scout ships on *Rescue Two* made sure everything was ready and perfect. So when Chairman Ray gave the order, a hundred thousand small explosions punctured the Void Space Bubble at the same time, allowing regular space to fill the void without destroying the ships inside.

And suddenly all the ships, most ancient looking, were back in real space, surrounded by a fleet of modern ships, both Seeder and Gray.

Tammy knew how those inside those old ships felt right now, going from being stuck with a lot of other ships and not being able to communicate with them or get their own ships working, to suddenly being surrounded by massive numbers of very modern ships.

But West had no idea.

Now, there sat the *Sky Fall,* the most famous missing ship in history, with over four million people on board.

And all of them very, very confused.

And soon to realize they were all very, very lost in time as well. The world all of them knew was just gone.

The future that they had set out to start had already come about.

West motioned that Tammy should join him and Chairman Ray in the first conversation with the Chairman of the *Sky Fall.*

Finding and rescuing lost ships was West's job. And he loved it more than he could admit.

But it wasn't really work.

Now that the rescue was done, the real work began with helping all the rescued get back to some sort of life in their new future.

And soon enough, West knew that he and his crew on *Rescue Two* would be back looking for more ships to save. West just hoped it would be sooner rather than later.

CHAPTER 14

It took them one month to finish helping with all the rescues from the bubble that had contained *Sky Fall* and so many other ships. For West, the month had not only not dragged by, but really sped by. Both he and Tammy got a lot better sense of what it was like to suddenly lose thousands if not millions of years.

West was surprised at how many made it through that. But he wasn't surprised at how much help the ones that didn't handle it well needed.

But now they were back out, with their huge list, scanning Void Space Bubbles.

And thankfully, the first few days all they found were empty bubbles.

The ship that was trapped inside a Void Space Bubble on the third day was so small the scans almost considered it debris and went past it. Tammy caught it and West was impressed. She put the scan up on the big screen and he still couldn't see a thing.

Neither could anyone else in the command center, which made him feel better.

"Okay, I give up," James, their chief engineer said from his station on the left.

"Me too," West said. "If there's something there I'm cooking dinner tonight."

"You're cooking," Tammy said, smiling. "Better be something good."

"Only if there's a ship there," West said.

Tammy just smiled and put a yellow arrow on the screen pointing to a tiny spot. Not in a million years would West have ever seen that.

"That's a ship?" James asked.

Tammy expanded out the image and got in closer and sure enough it was a small ship, shaped like a rocket with a pointed nose and fins around what looked like the base.

The inside of it more than likely had less room than was in this command center.

"Any kind of scan on it?" West asked.

"Three humans or Seeders," Tammy said. "Alive and seemingly fine. My guess is that they have been in there for about five days, so with the size of that bubble, about two million years our time."

West just shook his head. "Let's get them out of that bubble and on board, see what their story is."

And then he gave the general order to the seventeen around him on the command deck. "Search the local galaxies near where the bubble was when they got trapped. See if there are records of a ship like that being missing?"

Tammy shook her head. "Both galaxies near where the bubble was when they got trapped were in their early years of civilizations and space flight."

West just looked at her, his eyes wide.

"Early explorers?"

Tammy nodded.

"Early explorers" was a term used when young smart people on a seeded world discovered Trans Warp drive. Usually no one would believe them on their planet, so they built a ship themselves and tested it themselves.

In a small galaxy of say four-hundred-thousand seeded Earths, one in fifty of the Earths had early explorers. Most never got lost like this one. Although he knew a good percentage of them were killed by one thing or another, mostly their crudely made ship exploding or being hit by debris.

West had always had a lot of respect for early explorers from any planet. The courage it took to build a ship that could survive in space, then test an engine that no one had ever tested because it had to be tested in space.

He was looking forward to meeting these three.

"Never mind on that search," West said to the crew. "If they are early explorers, there will be no records after two million years."

"If you don't mind," Cynthia said from her station, "I'm going to try anyway while they are being freed from the bubble."

"Give it a shot," West said.

"And search the systems that are on the outer edge of the galaxy closer to where the bubble was located at that time."

"Thanks," Cynthia said.

They had saved ships with millions on board. For some reason, West felt more excited about this ship with just three.

And he had no idea why.

CHAPTER 15

It took about an hour for Ben and his team to basically pop the Void Space Bubble.

"Take us right to them," West said.

He knew that from their perspective, a massive ship just appeared beside them.

"Get a tractor beam on the ship and get it in one of the bays."

"They have got to be scared to death," Tammy said, shaking her head.

"Possible to break into their com system and get me on screen?" West asked.

"So primitive, it makes it harder, but got it," Cynthia said. "Their names are Bobby Steat, Carolyn Haaus, and David Steat. Language is early standard English, so not a problem for the computer."

"One more thing," Tammy said, turning to smile at West. "They all have Seeder genes."

"Fantastic," West said.

Tammy nodded.

Seeder genes were not uncommon in newly seeded worlds. About one in one hundred thousand had the gene and after a certain age, if not fired up, it went dormant and the person lived a normal human lifespan. It would make dealing with these three so much easier since they had that gene.

"Do it," West said. "Open a channel to them."

He then faced forward as three terrified young faces glanced up from their instruments as he took over their main view screen.

"Hi, Bobby, David, and Carolyn. My name is Chairman Evan West of the Seeder ship *Rescue Two*. We have just freed you from what is called a Void Space Bubble. How long were you in there where your engine would not work?"

"Six days, seven hours," Bobby said, his voice clearly shaking.

West nodded and glanced at Tammy.

"Their planet has a twenty-eight hour day, so almost exactly the time I figured," Tammy said. "About two million of their years."

West turned back to the three young faces, all three scared and shocked but managing to hold it together, which impressed West even more.

"What did she mean by two million years?" Bobby asked.

"Time does not really exist in a Void Space Bubble," West

said, "so your six days in the bubble equated to two million years in universe time."

David just sat down on the floor and put his head in his hands.

Carolyn just kept shaking her head.

Bobby opened his mouth, but no words came out.

"We're going to bring your ship into one of our docking bays and then over lunch try to explain what we can while we get you some help. Welcome to the future. You will find it is a pretty great place."

With that West cut off the communication system.

"Keep an eye on them," he said to Cynthia. Then he looked at his wife. "You want to be with me to meet them?"

"Wouldn't miss it for the world," she said, smiling.

West thought the same exact thing.

Fifteen minutes later Tammy and Evan were both standing near the very small tubular-shaped ship that was standing on its fins and held in place by tractor beams.

The three young adventurers were climbing down a metal ladder on the outside of the ship.

West found it interesting that both he and Tammy wore jeans, running shoes, and silk shirts, while the three young explorers wore basically the same thing, except not silk shirts, but from the looks of it cotton.

All three were about five-six and all three had shades of brown hair that looked like it needed a good combing.

Bobby reached the ground first, glanced around the huge hangar deck, and came over to West and Tammy and bowed slightly. "Thank you for the rescue."

"That is what this ship does," West said. "The name of the ship is *Rescue Two."*

Bobby looked around again as the other two joined him. "This is massive."

"This is the smallest of fifty hangar decks we have on this ship," West said. "We carry a fleet of two thousand ships far larger than yours to set charges to destroy the Void Space Bubbles."

"Oh," was all Bobby could say to that. The other two just looked around, shaking their heads.

"We're going to get you to rooms onboard here," Tammy said, "so you can change clothes and freshen up and then in an hour we'll go for lunch and explain what we can."

"Can you take us back to our home world?" Bobby asked.

West nodded. Cynthia had checked and their home world was still in existence. "Yes, but let's talk about that over lunch."

With that West jumped all of them to a large suite with three rooms and three bathrooms.

"Your clothes and belongs have all been transported here," Tammy said, indicating the piles of things on a large table near a kitchen.

"On hour," West said. "We'll explain what we can."

Then he and Tammy jumped back to the command deck.

"Contact Chairman Ray," West said to Cynthia. "Tell him we have found three early explorers in a Void Space Bubble and need some professional help and some guides to get them through the next few years. And tell him all three have the Seeder gene."

So for the next hour, he and Tammy worked to figure out the course ahead to more Void Space Bubbles. But his mind was more on the three explorers. He had no doubt that at their age, he would not have had the courage to do what they had done.

Not even close.

CHAPTER 16

Tammy and West appeared back in the explorer's suite in one hour and all three seemed to have showered and changed clothes and combed their hair.

Then West jumped all five of them to a private dining room near the command center.

"Is the ship moving you around like that?" Bobby asked.

"We are called Seeders," West said. "We are an offshoot of humans and all Seeders can teleport. Some vast distances."

"And all Seeders live long lives," Tammy said.

"How can you speak our language," Carolyn asked.

Tammy smiled. "Actually you speak our language. Your planet was seeded by our ships about two million, six hundred thousand years ago. All Earth-liked planets were in your galaxy. And many thousands of other galaxies over millions of years."

All three just sat there, staring at her.

"How about some food," West said and brought up a menu in front of him and showed the three how to do the same. "Different names, but the basics of this place at lunch is burgers and fries and milkshakes. Salads are good too."

After they had all ordered basically the same burgers and fries and milkshakes, David said, "I am having a very hard time grasping what is happening."

"Understandable," Tammy said.

"So could you maybe give us the very short version of what Seeders are exactly and how you got started?"

So West did, talking about the First Galaxy and the millions of years it took the Seeders branch of humanity to figure out how to get to other galaxies, albeit slowly in those early years.

"How fast can you go between galaxies now?" Bobby asked.

"Minutes," West said. "Faster if we have to for some reason."

"Between galaxies?" David asked, his voice sounding totally stunned.

West nodded. "Using basically the same drive you three invented for your ship. Just far more advanced and stable."

"So how did you end up outside your galaxy?" Tammy asked.

"Unstable drive is the reason," Bobby said. "We couldn't turn it off and if we hadn't run into what you call a Void Space Bubble, there was no telling where we would have ended up."

"Over three weeks at our top speed," David said.

"We pretty much figured we were dead," Carolyn said.

West just shook his head. "You early explorers are a rare group. Seeders need more like you three."

"Exactly right," Chairman Ray said.

He had appeared just beside West wearing his normal slacks, silk shirt and loafers. His long gray hair hung straight down his back.

"David, Bobby, Carolyn," Tammy said. "I would like to introduce you to Chairman Ray. He sort of directs things around the Seeder Universe."

Ray nodded to all three.

All three didn't know what to do, so they sort of bowed.

"I know all this feels impossible and unbelievable at the moment," Ray said. "But we have people who have helped others like you get acclimated to their new time and place. In fact, Chairman West and Tammy and their fantastic crew to this point have rescued upwards of eleven million people trapped over millions of years in these bubbles."

West was shocked. He had no idea that their total had gotten that big.

"And once you have learned about the world you find yourself in," Ray said, "we hope you will all three decide to join us, since you all three have the Seeders gene. If you agree, it would just need to be activated."

All three nodded and Bobby managed to say, "Thank you."

"But first we're going to take them back to their home planet," West said. "Let them complete their mission, even though there was a couple-million-year burp in the middle."

"Great idea," Ray said. "Congratulations on a successful

mission and doing what no one on your planet in your time would think of doing. I hope we meet again at some point."

With that he was gone.

"Does he teleport to another ship?" Carolyn asked.

"He is the chairman with his wife of a large mother ship," West said, "about a hundred times bigger than this ship. But I think at the moment it is about thirty galaxies away from here. He can teleport very, very long distances, but he is also almost six million years old."

All three early explorers just had their mouths open, staring at West.

"A lot of the people on missing ships we have been rescuing are his old friends and family he thought he had lost millions of years ago," Tammy said.

"My head hurts," Carolyn said.

"Yeah," West said, smiling. "All this will do that to you. Next stop an observation lounge."

A moment later all five of them were standing in front of a large viewport. All it showed was the intense blackness of space between galaxies and a number of galaxies in the distance.

"James," West said into the air. "Take us to our three guests' home world."

"Got it, Chairman," James said, his voice coming from the air.

"Watch that spiral galaxy right there," Tammy said, pointing. "That is your home galaxy."

As they watched, the galaxy grew and within fifteen seconds it filled the entire viewport and then a moment later they were in orbit over their guests' home world.

"We're actually home," Carolyn said, her voice a whisper. "But we have no family."

"In two million of your years," West said, "your planet settled into a very stable society and is part of a sector-wide trade alliance with about eight hundred other planets."

"All human," Bobby asked.

"All human and all seeded," Tammy said.

"No aliens?" David asked.

"Aliens live in other galaxies," Tammy said, "but we only seed galaxies without alien sentient life. So only human life. And Seeders helping out."

"Do they know you exist?" Carolyn asked.

"They all have discovered that they were all seeded on the planets by a long, lost race called the Seeders," West said. "They have no idea we are still around helping where we can. And in almost all galaxies, we keep it that way."

"Wow," David said.

"James," West said. "Take us back out to the rendezvous point with *Sunshine Stars*."

"We're going to transfer you and your ship to *Sunshine Stars*, which is a seeder mother ship with over a million souls on board," Tammy said. "You'll have a great place to live there and they will be with you as you want to explore your home world and get acclimated to the modern world."

"Each of you will have a counselor guide to help you," West said. "I'm afraid we have to get back to our mission of saving lost ships in those bubbles."

"But as Chairman Ray said, I hope we meet again."

"I'd love to be on a rescue mission like yours," Bobby said.

The other two agreed.

"How about in a few years," West said, "after you three get your feet under you and become Seeders, we talk. I just might have room for a few more really smart, adventurous crew."

All three said they would like that.

West shook all their hands, Tammy hugged each one.

And as West and Tammy transported back to the command center, the *Sunshine Stars* huge mother ship appeared.

"Tell them they have three good ones coming on board," West said.

"Already doing that," Tammy said.

"Then, James, after they are settled in over there, set course for the next bubble and let's see what we can find."

"With pleasure," James said.

And West completely agreed to that.

CHAPTER 17

Sitting at his kitchen table in his and Tammy's apartment, West studied the list of remaining lost ships. Tammy was busy on a project, so he was eating lunch alone.

They had rescued so many ships over the last few years, and had so many more to go.

Thousands and thousands and thousands more ships to go.

It sometimes seemed like an impossible task. Ships had been going missing for millions and millions of years. They had just vanished into Void Space Bubbles.

He put the list to one side, finished the last bite on his chicken sandwich, then picked up his dishes and put them in the sink. He was eating alone today because Tammy still had calculations to run and he didn't want to break her train of thought. So he had made her a sandwich as well, wrapped it and put it in the fridge for her to eat later.

As he finished the dishes, he stopped and looked around, something he didn't do that often in their busy life. He loved their apartment, the largest on the ship. A perk he got for being the Chairman. They had decorated it in brown tones and books. Both of them loved to read and also they both had an office here, plus a master bedroom that felt far too large. It had its own living room and furniture inside the master suite.

He left Tammy a note about the sandwich when she came out of her office in case he forgot to tell her, then picked up the lost ship list. There was still one ship on the list given to him by Chairman Ray that worried him. The name of the ship was the *Orange Sun.* It was a massive early generation mother ship.

A couple hundred years after it launched, it had contacted the first galaxy and informed them that a disease was spreading through the ship, something they had never seen before.

Just under a million people were on that ship.

And then suddenly the ship went silent.

Vanished.

The *Orange Sun* became known as the plague ship, even though Seeders were immune to everything. No one really knew what caused the problem, why the ship had vanished, or anything.

Searches over the millions of years had found no sign of the ship, so West figured one of three things happened. As they got sick, they just set the ship on autopilot and it kept going while everyone on board was killed by a mysterious disease.

Or they all left the ship for a planet's surface to form a colony and perished over time.

Or they hit a Void Space Bubble and were still in the middle of fighting the plague that hit them.

Plagues on Seeder ships almost never happened and when they did they were easily solved and stopped. It was why no humans were allowed on a Seeders ship. When a human was known to have Seeder genes and the genes were activated, not only would that person live a long time, be able to teleport, but also had intense immunity against almost anything.

West could not remember being sick one day since he became a Seeder.

But *Orange Sun* had been a Seeder ship. So what had hit them was something intense and very special. Lots of theories over the years had come forward about what the plague had been, but until someone found the ship, there were no set answers.

So he and Tammy had decided they would go looking for it.

Finding lost ships was their mission, after all.

She had spent four days looking for solutions as to where the plague ship might be. It had been lost for just over four million years, so she had tracked a dozen Void Space Bubbles that might have been along its original path and then located them where they were today after drifting for that long.

She also took the speed that the *Orange Sun* had been traveling and projected that over the millions of years. Frighteningly enough, the speed with the big old ship was slow enough that it would only take *Rescue Two* ten days to cover the same distances.

Then she eliminated the second alternative, that they had found an M-class planet and formed a colony. Every possible galaxy that had been close to them when they vanished had been seeded. Scout ships would have found the ruins and remains of the big ship, so *Orange Sun* didn't do that.

It took them just ten days to scan and destroy all the Void Space Bubbles the Orange Sun might have gotten trapped in.

Nothing but a Seeder scout ship that had gone missing just over two million years ago.

"So we are down to one option," West said to the seventeen on the command deck of *Rescue Two*. "Our job is to find out what happened to lost ships. So we chase *Orange Sun* on their original course and check and every bubble along the way that they might have run into. Tammy, put on the screen their possible courses."

A large V-shape appeared on the big screen.

"The point of the V is their last known position," Tammy said. "The green line up the middle of the V is if they did not vary their last reported course and speed."

West nodded.

"All other lines are logical course changes considering their last reported position from that original point."

West nodded again. "About how many Void Space Bubbles are inside that V?"

"Only counting the ones that would have been possible that *Orange Sun* might have encountered considering galactic movement," Tammy said, "just over two thousand."

"We'll scan all of them," West said. "Rescue the ships we find along the way and keep moving. If we have to go all the way out, this will take a few months. So let's get started."

Everyone around the command center nodded and went back to work.

And the search began.

CHAPTER 18

West contacted Chairman Ray and told him what they were doing and that if they did find the ship he should have medical people standing by who were experts in plagues.

Something besides a bubble had happened to this ship and his job was to find the ship, not deal with it.

Ray said he would have them standing by.

So as two months went by, they found seven other lost ships from various time periods and rescued them from the Void Space Bubbles.

And West's list of lost ships got seven smaller.

But still no sign of the *Orange Sun* mother ship.

Along the way West and Tammy had talked to numbers of experts about what kind of condition the *Orange Sun* might be in, besides the plague, after traveling for so many millions of years.

Assuming the shields had held, the condition would be good.

So just over two months after they had left on this search, West said, "Let's jump to where they would be if they had stayed on their original course and speed from the last reported position."

Tammy looked over at him from her station and nodded. They really had no more hope that the ship had got trapped by a bubble.

"Going now," James said. "Ten minutes at full speed."

"Keep scanners at full in all directions," West said. "I don't want to overshoot them."

He wasn't sure why he was calling *Orange Sun* a "them" because if it was out here, there was no them left. It was just a ship.

The ten minutes crawled by as everyone in the command center just did their job, not talking.

Then Tammy said simply, "I got it."

West stood from his command chair. "On screen."

"Right where it should be," Tammy said, shaking her head as she studied her screens.

Then an image came up at first showing just a dot, but within seconds they caught up to it and paced the big mother ship.

A large, older-style Seeders mother ship.

It had been one of the first dozen built in the early days of Seeding other galaxies.

"Scan it," West said, knowing that more than likely dozens of scans were already working on areas of the massive ship.

"Holy shit," someone said from the back.

Then Tammy said softly, "Not possible."

"What is not possible?" West asked.

"There are over a million souls on that ship," Tammy said, "all alive and seemingly healthy."

West just stood there and stared at her.

She looked up and nodded, a haunted look in her eyes.

"Do they know we are out here?" West asked.

"No," James said. "They have no command center, no communications, nothing. All destroyed in what looks to be a major event that took out almost all the significant control systems on the ship. Environment, gravity, food reproduction, power, are all fine."

West just shook his head, trying to get himself to imagine what he was being told.

"They have been flying totally blind for over five million years," Tammy said.

"Go back through as many records on their ship as you can access," West said. "Find out about the plague and how they managed this. I need to talk with Chairman Ray. This has just gone a long ways above our pay grade."

He signaled Tammy should join him and they jumped to their apartment. He contacted Ray and asked him if he could jump to them, or was it too far?

"That important?" Ray asked.

"We found *Orange Sun* and it is still occupied and not in a bubble."

"What?" Ray asked. Then he said, "I'll jump a few galaxies closer and then make the jump to you. About five minutes."

"Let's go get information for him," West said.

"And for me," Tammy said. "I'm still not believing this was possible."

"That makes two of us," West said.

A moment later they were back in the command center and working as more and more information poured in from all the scans.

CHAPTER 19

They had a lot of questions answered when Chairman Ray showed up standing behind West. Ray had been alive when the *Orange Sun* had launched and then vanished.

He always wore tan slacks, a silk shirt, and left his long, gray hair fall straight down his back and today was no exception.

And image of the *Orange Sun* was on the big screen in front of West's command chair.

Ray just stared at it for a long moment, then said, "Never thought I would see her again after the plague scare and then she vanished."

He turned to West. "What happened?"

"They were fighting the plague that seems from the records to be Sanction Fever," West said.

"That's what a lot of medical doctors thought it might be," Ray said, still staring at the ancient ship on the screen.

"From the records we found, they got it contained and a cure manufactured," Tammy said. "But then something went horribly wrong."

"Command center exploded," Ray said. "Took out their communications, and ability to stop or steer or even see where they were going."

"How did you know?" West asked, staring at Ray.

"We had two other accidents like that before we solved the flaw and fixed all the ships we could get to," Ray said. "*Orange Sun* was scheduled to be fixed after they got to their destination galaxy and settled into seeding."

West nodded. Now it all made sense.

"How did they stay alive over five million years?" Ray asked.

"There are none of the original crew still alive that we can find," Tammy said. "Most everyone of the original crew died after a few thousand years."

"Oh, god," Ray said, looking back at West and Tammy. "Are there any Seeders even left on board?"

"No," West said. "They are all human, living at best seventy or eighty years."

"This crew is seventy thousand generations removed from the original crew," Tammy said. "They have forgotten their origin and the ship is their entire world."

Ray just shook his head, staring at the big ship on the screen, clearly in shock.

"They are ruled by a royal family and professions are

passed down in ship upkeep like royalty," Tammy said. "Most of the crew live to serve the royalty and have babies. But overall it seems a happy, productive place."

"They have created great grass ball fields on the hangar decks," West said, "and giant parks. And education and the arts seem to be a high priority at all levels."

Ray just stood and shook his head slowly. Then he turned to West, his eyes serious. "How much longer can the *Orange Sun* keep going?"

"James," West said, turning to his chief engineer and navigator.

James shrugged. "Shields are holding fine, engines are holding fine, environmental systems are being maintained, as well as food replicators. So *Orange Sun* could keep going for another five millions years. Maybe longer, but it would depend on if they are going to hit something along the way."

Ray nodded. "I'll set up a ship to check on *Orange Sun* every hundred years or so. And we'll have lots of ships pacing it at times to study what has happened in there."

West just stared at Ray. "You're just going to let them go on?"

"Until we can't," Ray said, nodding. "Their world is that ship. If the ship starts to fail, we'll relocate them at that point. But they are an alien culture, a culture we did not seed and maintain. So our policy is to just let them live and go onward."

West started to object, then shut his mouth. He had not one clue what to do with over a million humans who had never seen the outside of a massive ship. Chairman Ray clearly did know exactly how to deal with them.

"Good work, everyone," Ray said to the entire command center.

Then he vanished.

The shocked silence filled the command center.

"Keep researching and doing scans and sending it back," West said, "so those headed out here to watch and study this ship will have a head start.

Around the large command center heads nodded, but the silence still just held.

"Tammy and I are going to figure out where our next possible lost ship is at," West said. "And as Chairman Ray, said, great work everyone."

With that, West jumped him and Tammy back to their kitchen.

"I have our next target bubble all ready to go," Tammy said.

"I know," West said. "But I need to let everyone have the time to let this failure sink in. And see why Chairman Ray was right."

"Failure?" Tammy asked.

West nodded. "We found the ship, sure. But we couldn't rescue the ship or the people in it."

"But at least now it won't be called a plague ship," Tammy said.

"There is that," West said. "But now what would you call it?"

Tammy had no answer to that question.

And neither did he.

CHAPTER 20

West stood near his command chair, sipping a cup of coffee, his second cup of the day, and staring at the big screen in front of him with information from scans flowing across it almost too fast to read.

But he knew what he was looking for and he had a hunch they were going to find the ship they were looking for.

What to do with *Nebula Four* when they found it was another matter altogether.

This time they would have no crew trying to grasp the vast numbers of years the mother ship had lost, but once they released the Void Space Bubble, they would have a massive mother seeder ship on automatic pilot, and no real way to get into it or shut it down.

Yup, the *Nebula Four* was a ghost ship.

Around him the large control center of *Rescue Two* worked in silence, the seventeen crew were all busy over their stations. Even the persistent coffee smell seemed to have faded some.

Tammy, at the station closest to his own, had found the Void Space Bubble that held the big ghost ship.

This bubble was now outside any normal traffic lines between Seeders' galaxies, but at one point almost four million years ago, it was right on a path that Seeders of that time had sent five unmanned mother ships ahead, hoping that newly seeded galaxies would have enough Seeders by that time to man the millions needed on each mother ship.

It worked for four of the big ships sent ahead, but one ship vanished in the thousand-year journey.

Maybe today they would solve another mystery.

Finally the scan data stopped that had been filling the big screen in front of West.

Tammy looked over at him.

"Found the *Nebula Four*."

A cheer went up through the command center, but West didn't see his wife smiling as she would normally.

"What else is in there?" he asked.

Tammy shook her head. "Not sure. Looks like a human ship, but it can't be."

"It's an Ancient's mother seeder ship," Carolyn said from the back top row of the command center.

Silence instantly filled the command center as everyone turned to stare at her.

Carolyn was an Ancient who had decided to stay with the

Seeders and help out when the Ancient's vanished to a new homeland a few hundred years before. No one really knew where the Ancients went.

But it had been the Ancients that had seeded what Seeders called "The First Galaxy."

There were rumors that the Ancients had seeded other galaxies, but no one knew where. Seeders now had seeded over a hundred thousand galaxies, and no signs of any previously seeded galaxies.

"Any idea how long it has been trapped in the bubble?" West asked, glancing at Carolyn, then back at his wife.

"This is a huge bubble," Tammy said. "So for them the difference in their time and our time would be large, very large."

"About forty million years," Carolyn said from the back, her voice hushed. "From the readings I am getting, that is the *StarEater*. It disappeared and became legend to the Ancients forty million years ago."

"Oh, shit," West said. "So we found the *Nebula Four,* but still have no way to get inside it and stop it."

Tammy nodded.

"And we found an Ancient's mother ship called the *StarEater*." West looked back at Carolyn. "Any idea how many on board that ship?"

"Thirty-one million," Carolyn said.

Gasps from around the room.

Tammy was nodding. "It is a good hundred times larger than *Nebula Four*."

"Oh, great," West said. "An empty run-a-way ship and a ship carrying more people than a small planet could support. Any more surprises?"

Thankfully, the command center was quiet at that question.

CHAPTER 21

West glanced at Tammy. "Meeting room, please. Carolyn, would you join us?"

He jumped to their meeting room just off the command center. Tammy and Carolyn arrived just a second later.

The room was a pretty standard meeting room, with a long table and about ten chairs. It was decorated in brown tones, had hidden view screens, and pictures actually hung in frames on the walls, of planets and nebulas and other beautiful sites from around the galaxies.

"I wanted you both here when I told Chairman Ray what we had found."

Then West turned and looked up slightly. "Chairman Ray, could you please join me in our meeting room when you have a moment?"

Less than five seconds later Ray appeared. He had on his

standard tan slacks, button-down dress shirt, and loafers. His long gray hair was perfectly straight running down his back.

West knew he had teleported here from two galaxies away.

"Tammy. Carolyn. Nice seeing you both again," Ray said.

They both smiled and nodded back.

"We found the *Nebula Four*," West said.

"Five million years ago I gave up hope of ever seeing that ship again," Ray said, shaking his head. "Great work. I'll get *BlueBird* mother ship here in a few hours and they'll work to get inside once you release it from the bubble and then work to get it refurbished. We should be able to still use it for in-galaxy missions."

West nodded, then said, "We found something else in the bubble as well."

Ray looked puzzled, then glanced at Carolyn who he knew was an Ancient and said, "An Ancient's ship?"

Carolyn nodded. "We found the *StarEater*."

"Oh, shit," Ray said. "That's an Ancient's mother ship."

West nodded. "Been in there for over forty million years. Thirty-one million people on board."

Ray's mouth was just open as he tried to digest the news.

"My best estimate is that seven weeks have passed for them," Tammy said.

"Won't matter," Carolyn said. "The entire thirty-one million are in deep sleep and the course is set on autopilot."

West just shook his head. "So basically we are freeing two ships on autopilot and no way to get into either of them. Am I right about that at the moment?"

Ray and Carolyn nodded.

Tammy just looked at him, shaking her head.

Ray finally turned to Carolyn. "Can you tell me where to find some of the oldest Ancients who stayed behind like you to help us out?"

"No idea, I'm afraid, Chairman."

Ray nodded and thanked her for her help. Then he turned to West.

"Get what information you can on both ships, but don't let them out yet until I get back here with some Ancients, since this is their ship. And get some mother ships ready to help out as well with our lost ship."

With that, he vanished.

The three of them went back to the command center and West told everyone what Ray had said.

Then he and Tammy jumped to their apartment to get lunch and try to talk all this through, if there was much to talk through.

CHAPTER 22

The *BlueBird* mother ship arrived in two hours, just as Ray said it would. West and Tammy went over to talk with their two chairman and fill them in on what else had been found.

Five of the over one million crew on *BlueBird* were Ancients and West invited them over to the *Rescue Two* to talk and work with Carolyn. All five were stunned that *StarEater* had been found after over forty million years. To Ancients, West was starting to realize that it seemed to be a very mythological ship.

So the five agreed to join Carolyn and work on scanning the massive ship, as best they could with it frozen in a Void Space Bubble.

Then nothing happened for almost two full days.

There was only so much information they could get through a Void Space Bubble, but Carolyn and the other five ancients basically had a diagram of the massive ship, how many other ships were on board, where most of the population of the ship slept, and so on.

They also figured out that the original trip was to last fifty thousand years in cold sleep and the original galaxy goal was far outside the range that the Seeders had claimed so far.

West hated just waiting, but there was no choice. Whatever they did with the two ships, they had to do it right. And that meant waiting.

Then right after lunch on the third day, Chairman Ray appeared beside West on the command deck and at the same time, an Ancient's transport ship appeared. It was tiny compared to the two Seeders ships.

Then within the next two minutes, six huge Seeders mother ships appeared and stood back and away from the Void Space Bubble.

"Two from the Ancients' ship asking permission to come aboard," Ray said. "In the meeting room."

West nodded and he and Tammy and Ray met Carolyn and the other five Ancients in the meeting room. A moment later two others appeared. Both had gray hair, something West seldom saw on any Seeder or Ancient except for Ray.

They both bowed to Carolyn, which surprised West more than he wanted to let on.

Ray indicated that they should all sit around the table and they did.

Ray introduced the two new arrivals, but West knew he would never either remember them or pronounce their names correctly.

Then Ray turned to him. "What have you found with your scans?"

West indicated that Carolyn should take the question.

"It is, without a doubt, the *StarEater*," she said. "The ship we have been looking for. All its systems seem to be functioning perfectly and none of the crew were disturbed due to the bubble. All are still sleeping and so far there have been no fatalities."

"Is there a way to get inside and wake up the crew, maybe a few thousand at a time?" Ray asked.

"No," Carolyn said.

West looked around and every Ancient in the room was nodding to that blunt statement.

"So do you have a suggestion as to what we should do?" Ray asked.

"We let them out of the bubble and let them continue their journey," Carolyn said. "They will wake in thirty-five thousand years, even if they are off course. We will be there to help them when they wake."

West just sat there, his mouth open.

"Any other idea to stop them or awaken them now would be too dangerous, I assume?" Ray asked.

Again every Ancient in the room nodded.

"Besides," Carolyn said. "If we did that, their mission would be a failure. We need to let them complete their mission, even if we help them at the end."

West glanced around the table and it was clear that every Ancient's head was again nodding in agreement.

Ray took a deep breath and sighed. "Give word that the

mother ships, except for *BlueBird,* can return to their former missions."

"I'll do that," Tammy said and vanished.

West knew she was going to be happy they were gone because she was worried that no one knew in what direction those autopiloted ships were going to emerge when they blew the bubble.

Then Ray turned to West. "Have your team release them from the bubble. We'll watch from here in the conference room."

West nodded and jumped back to the command center.

"Get them out of there, but safely," he ordered to Ben. "Millions of lives are at stake."

"We got it," Ben said.

So over the next hour everyone checked their calculations twice again, the same calculations that had been gone over a dozen times in the last two days. For if they blew the Void Space Bubble wrong, it would destroy both ships.

Finally, on West's order, he got the *Rescue Two* and *BlueBird* backed way away and the Void Space Bubble lit up for a fraction of a second and then vanished, leaving two large ships on autopilot heading off into space.

BlueBird turned and followed *Nebula Four* while no one followed *StarEater*. Its path was exactly known the moment the bubble was popped and an Ancient ship and a Seeder ship would check in on it regularly over the next thirty-five thousand years.

West and his crew had dealt with vast amounts of time, but

thinking about just waiting for a ship's crew just to wake up in thirty-five thousand years was just amazing.

Chairman Ray appeared on the command deck and thanked them all for the great work and he was excited to see what they would find next.

Rescue Two jumped to a spot near *BlueBird* and let the five Ancients teleport back.

Then West and Tammy asked Carolyn to dinner in their apartment. West really needed to figure out why they had all bowed to her.

So over salads and before steaks, he finally asked her.

She laughed. "Because we found *StarEater.* Even though we all did, but as an Ancient, I get the honor of being the Ancient that found the fabled lost ship."

West shook his head. "Were the two that arrived far older than you?"

"Millions of years older," she said. "I am a new generation Ancient."

"So it seems," West said, shaking his head, "that Ancients have a lot of beliefs and customs that we Seeders don't know about."

Carolyn just smiled and then said, "Oh, you have no idea."

And with that West decided it was better to just have a nice dinner and changed the topic. After all, there was time.

Lots of time, it seemed.

CHAPTER 23

"Where did they go?"

West wanted an answer and he wanted it now. To be honest, it scared him to not have an answer.

Around him the seventeen command crew on the command deck all were intent at their stations, focused, trying to answer his question. The air in the large command center seemed to stop moving, the sounds gone.

He had a fresh coffee in his hand and he put it down on the arm of his command chair, not even thinking about it.

Tammy seemed to be the most intense at her station close to his command chair and he had a hunch she was the one that was going to find the answer.

On the screen in front of them was a Seeders mid-sized ship named *Heavens Day* that originally, five million years before, had a crew of over forty thousand souls run by

Chairman Allan Holland. It now floated in space in front of them, completely empty.

No crew, no bodies, nothing.

Just empty.

Not possible.

Where had the crew gone?

They had just freed the ship from a very large Void Space Bubble, so Tammy had estimated the ship had been in the bubble for five million years regular time, but only about six days in the bubble itself.

And no signs of small ships in the bubble at all, so West was guessing that ship went into the bubble empty.

So even though Seeder records were not that great over the millions of years, the records had no records of the ship being lost.

Not even a hint of it.

Tammy had traced where the bubble in area of the disappearance might have drifted to over all that time and instead of finding a ship they were hoping to find, they had found *Heavens Day*.

Empty.

"Anyone?" West said to his crew. "Any record of those forty thousand people being rescued?"

A few heads shook, everyone kept working.

Finally Cynthia said, "No record of it even being missing."

West turned back to look at the big view screen that filled one entire front wall of the command center. As far as the ship was concerned, it had been empty for only seven days.

The ship had a pretty good forward sub-light speed momentum, but no engines working.

West turned to his chief engineer at a station on his left. "James, any evidence of problems with the ship? Engines, plague, environmental controls? Anything?"

James was a young-looking man with freckles and red hair who had a brain of a genius and could keep anything running. He actually was over four hundred years old.

"Nothing," James said. "All systems, including life support and drive are fully functioning. It seems that everyone just teleported away. All lifeboats and secondary ships on their decks are still in place and working fine as well."

"Can you tell how long the ship drifted empty in space before hitting the bubble?"

"Best guess," James said. "Maybe between a thousand and five thousand years. I would know more if I could get into the ship."

"Why would forty thousand Seeders just teleport away?" West asked, his stomach twisting even more. "Full families. Everyone."

"Maybe they were not given a choice," Tammy said, looking up from her board.

West looked into his wife's eyes and he could tell she was just as worried as he was.

James said, "We need to get hooked into their systems and get answers before we make another move."

West agreed. No telling what they were facing with this.

He turned to James. "Take a team, as many as you need to

get answers, everyone in full protective gear. No slips. Let me know when you are ready to jump over there."

James nodded and vanished from his station.

Normally Seeders have full protection from anything, on any planet they might visit, but West had no memory of hearing about a ghost ship before, besides one that had launched empty. Seeder crews just didn't vanish.

He turned back to his crew circled at stations around his command chair in three levels. "Someone research the history of Seeder ghost ships."

"I have been, sir," Cynthia said. "There are none that weren't launched empty ahead of time. Until now."

He nodded and turned back to stare at the ghost Seeders ship floating in space in front of him. What the hell happened?

And where did the forty-thousand souls on board vanish to?

CHAPTER 24

Ten very long minutes later, James contacted West.

"Taking twenty with me. We are in full protective suits and ready to jump."

"Good luck," West said.

West then said to the crew around him. "Put up on the screen the layout in three-D of the plans of that ship and where each of our people are at. Keep a very close eye on them and their vital signs."

A moment later the three-dimensional image of the entire *Heavens Day* and all the decks appeared on the screen and a moment later twenty-one white dots.

Looked like James took ten to the command center, sent four to engineering, four to look at the other ships on the hangar deck, and three to explore personal quarters.

"Systems coming up on the *Heavens Day,*" Candice reported. "No problems at all."

After five minutes, it looked like James and the crew on the command center had the ship completely active.

"Chairman," James said. "All systems are functioning fine. The ship drifted without crew for just over two thousand years before hitting the bubble. Sending details of sub-light drift speed and what the area around the ship looked like."

"Got it," Tammy said.

West glanced over at Tammy who was working away at her station faster than he had seen her move in some time. She had the computer power to figure out the float over five million years of a Void Space Bubble through all the galaxy movements, and with the information that Andy had just sent her, she would be able to figure out where the crew might be, if still alive after five million years.

At least they would know where they went.

After another thirty seconds, Tammy said, "Got them."

Up on the screen came an image of a small cluster galaxy and a blinking light right at the edge of the galaxy.

"That galaxy is marked alien life and should be avoided." Tammy said.

"When was it marked that?" Evan asked.

"Six million years ago," Tammy said. "One million years before *Heavens Day* crew vanished."

West just wanted to be sick. No Seeders interacted with aliens besides the Gray. When a galaxy was discovered to have a sentient race, the Seeders just marked it stay away and went around. There were more than enough galaxies without any form of sentient life to seed.

"James?" West asked. "Were the shields up when the ship was left?"

"Yes," James said.

West nodded. A Seeder's ship shields could bore a hole through a planet and come out the other side without damage. Running into a sun would destroy the ship, but not much else.

West turned to his wife. "As best you can, would the ship have ever been found if it hadn't run into the bubble?"

"No," Tammy said. "The course it was on would have drifted it away from all possible Seeder inhabited space."

West nodded. The crew of the ship had not wanted to be found. They had not wanted *Heaven's Day* to ever be found, either.

It was time for help.

Evan looked up slightly and then said, "Chairman Ray. Could use your help when you get a moment, please."

Ray was alive when this ship went missing. West wanted to know why it was not on their missing ships list, and why the crew of that ship didn't want to be found.

With luck, Ray would know the answer.

CHAPTER 25

Chairman Ray appeared less than a minute later. He was dressed in his normal slacks, silk shirt, and loafers. His long gray hair was straight down his back.

"Thank you for coming," West said.

"Your mission of finding lost ships and many of my lost friends is always my first priority," Ray said.

"Well," West said. "We might not always find good things."

West turned to his crew. "Put the image of the *Heavens Day* back on the screen."

"Heavens Day?" Ray asked, clearly shocked.

"The first Seeder ghost ship that we can't find in the records," West said.

"Ghost ship?" Ray asked, staring at the image of the ship. "You mean the crew had completely vanished?"

"They left the ship about two thousand years before a

bubble got it," West said. "We don't know why, but we do know where they went."

"I know why," Ray said, softly. "Not sure it is a good thing to know where they went."

West looked directly at Ray. "The reason I assume is why this ship was not on our missing ship list?"

Ray nodded. "There are maybe a hundred more."

"Do we need to talk in private?" West asked.

Ray shook his head. "This is Seeder history. Better we stop covering it up, since you might find others."

West nodded. "What do you want to do with *Heavens Day?*"

"I'll be back in about an hour and get a mother ship here to take care of it. I will need help explaining the history."

Then Ray vanished.

"James," West said. "Put everything on standby and bring everyone back. Go through decontamination just in case."

"On our way," James said.

"Plot in a course to where you think they might be," West said to Tammy. "How long will it take us to reach it?"

"Two hours and fifteen minutes," she said. "Any idea at all what this is all about?"

"Not a clue," West said. "But when it comes to Seeder history, it is never pretty."

One hour later, Ray and a man who introduced himself as Andrew, a Seeder historian arrived. He looked like a historian, with large glasses, balding head, and a round figure. West didn't even know there was such a thing as a Seeder historian.

Shortly after they arrived, the *Diving Dove* Seeder mother

ship appeared next to *Heavens Day* and began to bring it into one of their decks.

"A place we can go and broadcast to your entire crew?" Ray asked. "Since all of you will be dealing with this going into the future."

West turned to Cynthia and she nodded that she would have it set up.

West, Tammy, Ray, and Andrew jumped to the conference room and took seats at the big conference table.

"Ready, Cynthia?" West asked.

"Cameras on all four of you. Open mike to the crew."

"Everyone," West said, "as best you can with what you are doing at the moment, pay attention and Chairman Ray and Andrew, a Seeder historian are going to give us some background about Seeder history and why *Heavens Day* was abandoned."

Ray indicated that Andrew should begin.

"In the early days of humanity in the First Galaxy, there were many factions. And as it became clear that Seeders could live longer lives and handle the issues of space better than humans, even more factions developed."

"It seems that in hindsight," Ray said, "the Ancients, who seeded what we call the First Galaxy, helped us gently through the rough times, which is why we always stay behind and help the worlds we seed."

West nodded. He knew this basic history.

"As we started to move to other galaxies and seed them," Andrew said, "there was a large faction of Seeders who did not like the methods we used. They wanted to just leave the

M-Class planets as we found them and form colonies and settle them."

"They also did not like that we wiped every planet clean as we started," Ray said, "and then recreated the same animals and humans from the same DNA over and over on every planet, making every planet basically Earth, a replica of the first Earth, with the exact same false history as the Ancients gave us."

"The differences between the two factions got so intense," Andrew said, "that it threatened to end all Seeding and colonization efforts. So basically groups of different sizes were given ships and they scattered off in all directions to colonize fresh M-class planets in any way they saw fit."

"How many ships were in that exodus?" West asked.

"Over about fifteen thousand years," Ray said, "sixteen hundred and five ships full of Seeders and humans left to colonize."

"So far we have discovered no successful colonies," Andrew said. "Most, over one thousand of the sixteen hundred, were wiped out by their new homes within two hundred years. Five we have found are existing at a barbaric level, but we are leaving them alone as we would do any alien race. That was their wish."

"And the others?" Tammy asked.

"No sign of any of the other three hundred and ten yet," Ray said. "Until you found *Heavens Day*."

"Do we have permission to see if we can find their colony?" West asked.

Ray nodded. "As long as, if any of them are still there and have built a colony, you stay hidden and away from them."

Andrew nodded. "That was our initial agreement with every ship. Unless they asked for help, we would leave them alone. Not one has asked for help."

West and Tammy asked a few more questions, then thanked Ray and Andrew for the information and the two men jumped away.

Tammy and West jumped back to the command center.

"Okay, everyone," West said to the entire crew. "Back to work. We're going to go see what happened to the *Heavens Day* crew five million years ago."

Evan knew that was most likely going to be impossible, but they had to look.

Two and a half hours later they reached the edge of the small cluster galaxy. Near the far edge of the galaxy, there were remains of what had been a pretty robust growing alien civilization that had gone out over a five-star system before falling into ruin and vanishing. It looked to West like it had been a hive mind race that looked a lot like raccoons.

West and his crew did careful scans of almost a hundred M-Class planets near the opposite edge of the small galaxy before finally finding faint remains of a human colony and a number of human satellites still orbiting in high, stable orbits.

"Chairman Ray," West said, looking up. "We found them."

Ray appeared beside West in the command center.

"Great work," Ray said.

"Looks like they lasted and grew for about fifty thousand

years," Tammy said, "after they first arrived here. They called their planet *A New Day*."

"Looks like they covered most of the planet at one point," James said. "Subsurface scans show a detailed road system and lots and lots of remains of major cities all over the planet."

West was shocked because the planet was lush and green and had three large oceans. "What happened?"

"More than likely the same thing that would happen to millions of the planets we seed if we didn't stay around and help them," Ray said. "Each planet gets to a point that it has the weapons to destroy itself. Most do, sadly, unless stopped or guided. It is a human trait and seemingly part of our evolution."

"How many planets that we seed are we not able to stop the self destruction no matter how hard we try?" Tammy asked.

Ray looked pained, then said, "We are not able to stop about one in ten."

West was shocked. But standing here in orbit, looking over the ancient remains of what clearly had been a large civilization, it was hard not to believe that kind of number.

"I'll get a couple of science research vessels here to study the colony," Ray said. "Find out more about it."

"And we'll get back to work searching for lost ships," West said.

"Thanks for the good work on this," Ray said. "Only three hundred and nine colonies still missing."

With that he vanished leaving command central in deadly silence.

"I like it much better when we find and rescue ships with people in them," Tammy said, breaking the silence.

There was agreement from almost everyone in the command center.

"So let's go find some people to rescue," West said. "Tammy, give James the course to the next Void Space Bubble on our list."

"Gladly," Tammy said.

West slumped into his command chair and for just a few minutes more he stared at the green planet below them that had swallowed a human civilization millions of years earlier.

Considering the odds against any civilization, it was stunning any had made it.

And he most definitely agreed with Tammy. It was a lot more fun to rescue live people.

SECTION THREE

RESCUE THREE

CHAPTER 26

Chairman Kait Paddy and her wife, Chairman Mora Thomas stood beside their command chairs, facing the command crew of fifty that stood near their stations on the massive four-tiered command center of the *Distant Star*.

The *Distant Star* was built like a Seeder's mother ship, yet their mission was not to seed another galaxy with humanity, but to see if they could reach an edge to the universe, if that was even possible.

Kait thought it possible and believed in the mission, much more than Mora. But Mora had agreed and after a year of preparations, Kait actually thought she was excited.

Kait looked out at the silent command center, then smiled at Mora, who nodded. "We left just forty-six days ago from the First Galaxy," Kait said, "the galaxy where this wave of humanity started to expand into the thousand galaxies that it covers now."

"Scout ships have explored the galaxies beyond the edge of seeded space," Mora said, "looking for good new homes for humanity to expand into over time."

"But right as we speak," Kait said to the entire command, "we have officially traveled farther than any Seeders ship on recorded history."

Cheering broke out among all the crew.

And that cheering made Kait smile. She and Mora had picked a great crew, of that she had no doubt. A crew that really wanted to explore.

"So let's get to work and see what we can find," Mora said. "Speed at two-thirds, make sure we don't miss any galaxy scans as we go by. Our job is to explore and map until we run out of universe to explore."

"And we won't know what we are looking for until we find it," Kait said. "Let's go have some fun."

With that, as the crew settled into their stations and back to work, Kait said to Mora, "Lunch?"

"Perfect," Mora said and a moment later they were back in their three-bedroom suite, standing in their kitchen.

Kait hugged Mora and then gave her a kiss. They fit so well together, it was amazing. Both six-foot tall, Kait had short brown hair, Mora long blond hair she kept pulled back while in the command center. They were both thin and both loved to exercise, mostly run. And considering that this ship held almost one million people including families, a normal sized crew for a Seeders mother ship, they had a lot of places to run, not counting virtual running tracks.

They had been a couple now for going on three hundred years and Kait loved Mora more now than when they first met, back before they knew they were Seeders, back before they were offered the position of being Chairmen of a Seeders mother ship.

Their apartment had a fantastic living room, furnished in what Mora called soft comfort and dressed up in brown and tan tones of everything.

One wall was filled with real paper books, and when they set up the ship, they even included a publishing press for books of all kinds.

They had three rooms off the main part, so they each had an office and then the master bedroom suite.

The kitchen was modern and Mora kept it well-stocked even though Kait loved to cook more than Mora. There was a large glass dining table off to one side of the kitchen that was often just covered in paper and electronic tablets.

Mora dug out iced tea for both of them as Kait worked on roast beef sandwiches. Then Mora got out some chips and they moved to the table to eat.

"I'm excited," Kait said. "Out here where no one has gone before."

"That we know of," Mora said.

Kait nodded to that, even though both of them knew it was unlikely since up until about three hundred years before, the speed of Seeder's ships was slow enough that it would have taken more millions of years than Seeders had been around to travel what they had done in just over six weeks.

Just no way for the human mind to understand the distance they traveled in just one day at two-thirds speed. They would go by at least eighty galaxies in that amount of time if they didn't stop to look at something.

Kait expected them to do a lot of stopping. And she was fine with that. Their mission was to explore. That was what they were going to do.

"Chairman needed in the command center," a voice said just as Kait took the last bite of her sandwich.'

"Well, that was fast," Mora said.

They both grabbed their glasses of iced tea and jumped back to the command center.

Their second in command was a man named James. He looked very young, yet was still hundreds of years old and had been the navigator for the century *Rescue Two* had searched for lost ships. He was a few thousand years younger than Kait and Mora and he was so battle tested, they trusted him completely.

"Passed five galaxies," James said. "All great candidates for seeding if humanity ever heads this direction."

Kait doubted it would, but they were sending back a constant stream of information, so there was no telling.

"We did spot a large ship in a Void Space Bubble," James said and indicated they should take a look at the screen.

"Like old home days, huh?" Kait said, and James just laughed.

"Clearly alien," James said, "more than likely a generation

ship, seems to have been in there for a couple of weeks their time, so millions of years have passed out here."

"Get *Rescue Three* out there and get ready to pop that bubble," Kait said. "Then we can get better scans of who they are and where they were headed before they got trapped. See if there is anything we can do to help them."

Kait and Mora sat in their command chairs and watched as the fourteen hundred crew of *Rescue Three,* based on *Distant Star,* did its work to safely destroy the Void Space Bubble without destroying the ship inside it.

Before they had started this mission, Kait and Mora had met with the legendary Chairman of *Rescue Two,* Chairman Evan West and his wife Tammy. And they had set up *Rescue Three* to be based on *Distant Star.*

Rescue Two was still working after almost eight hundred years, but finding less and less, so West and Tammy had suggested James, their second in command as Kait and Mora's second in command and navigator, and Ben in charge of the scout ships to pop the bubbles.

Both loved to explore, push the edges.

They all knew that past a certain point on the *Distant Star's* journey outward, they would only find alien ships in the bubbles, but it was critical to the history of an area of space to study those they found and release them safely.

So it didn't surprise anyone that they would find alien ships in the Void Space Bubble this far out. And numbers of the crew of *Rescue Three* had been trapped for long periods of time in a bubble and had wanted to help free others.

Rescue Three, based on *Distant Star* was the best solution.

So finally the two chairmen were asked for the order to rescue the alien ship and Kait looked at Mora, then said, "Ready to scan?"

"Ready," the answer came back from a few members of the command crew.

They both nodded and Mora said, "Do it."

Flashes of light at the exact same time showed the tiny explosions all around the space bubble and the alien ship appeared.

It had a long straw-shape to it and its engines were clearly in the empty center of the straw while the crew lived around the edges.

The straw seemed to be spinning giving gravity to anyone along the outside.

"It's a generation ship, all right," James said from his station off to their right. About a tenth of the size of *Rescue Three.*"

Kait just sat next to Mora and stared at the alien ship. Neither one of them had had any contact with any kind of alien race, since Seeders just avoided any galaxy that had aliens at any level inside it.

So this was a first for both of them.

"And they are ant-like," James said, "more than likely with hive mind culture. And they are all in cold sleep at the moment."

"Where did they come from?" Mora asked.

"Seems that that their original path was from a galaxy ahead of us," Elgin said, "but the drift of the bubble took them way off course. They were trying to reach a satellite galaxy of their home galaxy. But they have no faster than basic light drive, so this trip was scheduled to take two hundred thousand years."

"Can you tell if their ship is still solid and they are still alive?"

"It is," James said. "And they are."

"Any ideas?" Kait looked at her partner.

Mora just shrugged. "Have *Rescue Three* tow the ship to a place close to their intended galaxy target, set it on course, and let them go. Seems to be the least we can do for them."

Kait loved that idea. *Rescue Three* could catch up in a day or so.

"Let's do it."

Mora gave the order and then they sat there until *Rescue Three* had the alien ship carefully connected in a protective tractor beam and headed toward the alien ship's original target millions of years before. Compared to *Rescue Three,* the small stick of a ship looked tiny and fail.

It really gave Kait a perspective of what the Seeders did regularly that was actually very special.

"Let's get back on course," Kait said as she and Mora stood. "Well done, everyone. And make sure we give that home galaxy where they originated a distance. No telling what they have advanced in the millions of years."

Then she and Mora jumped back to their apartment to get changed into their exercise clothes.

Kait had a hunch that this was going to be the way the next numbers of years, maybe even decades would go.

And she had to admit, that wouldn't be bad at all.

SPECIAL BONUS CONTENT

The original short story, "Shadow in the City," which was inspired by a Janis Ian song, launched a universe so vast that many novels have followed. Read on for this special bonus content, as well as an additional bonus Seeders Universe short story, "A Matter for a Future Year."

Dean Wesley Smith

USA Today Bestselling Writer

In the dead city
Carey found a life
and a future.

SHADOW IN THE CITY

AUTHOR'S NOTE

"Shadow in the City" became the basis of the novel Dust and Kisses, *the prequel novel to the Seeders Universe series of novels.*

The story is based on the song lyrics of "Here in the City" by Janis Ian, written with permission for Stars Anthology *edited by Janis Ian and Mike Resnick.*

The lyrics this story is based on are reprinted here with permission from Janis Ian.

SHADOW IN THE CITY

"You don't see many shadows here in the city
Only picturesque windows, all covered and dirty
Black and grey that once was new
Yesterday that once was you
No, I can't find my shadow in the city"

"Here in the City"
Janis Ian

CHAPTER 1

She stood on the abandoned freeway overpass and stared at the gray of the dead city of Portland, Oregon, and the deep blue of the gently flowing river below her. Four years ago the city below her had died along with the rest of the world. So why had she picked today, of all days, to finally go back?

Carey Noack was five foot two and didn't have an extra ounce of fat on her body. Over the last four years she had kept her light-brown hair cut short and out of the way. Today, for the final hike into the center of the big buildings, she wore a black sleeveless T-shirt, jeans, and her favorite tennis shoes.

"Man, Carey, how stupid is this?" she asked herself as she used a small towel from her pack to wipe the sweat from her face and arms. The weather had turned out to be one of those typical Oregon summer days, where the bright sun and clear skies made the air feel warmer than it actually was. It seldom got above seventy degrees where she lived, overlooking the sandy beach and the pounding waves of the Pacific Ocean, making today feel even worse.

She finished wiping off her arms, put the towel back in her pack, and grabbed the water bottle.

"Better keep drinking this," she said out loud before taking a long, deep drink of the warm water. She was going to have to be careful, make sure she didn't push too hard. She hated heat, and the last thing she would need would be to get heat stroke now.

Standing there on the overpass, it was hard to push away the memories of nightmarish last days she had spent in the city, and the last trip to the coast. It had been hot that week as well. The dead, staring bodies had been everywhere, filling the hot winds with the smell of rotting flesh.

She had simply run, trying to get away from the death and the smell. Of course there had been dead bodies in the small towns on the coast as well, and it had taken her some time to find sanctuary. The house she had taken, just north of Depoe Bay, sat on a rock ledge jutting out into the ocean. The breezes were always off the water, and seldom did the smell of rotting flesh reach her.

Why, after four long years of living alone on the coast, was she back today, of all days?

Was she really that lonely? She knew that many, many nights, especially during the first year, she had simply sat and cried, trying to hold back the overwhelming feelings of sadness, shock, and loneliness. It was one thing to be a loner when the world was alive around her. It was another to be completely alone, talking to herself and her cats.

She missed her cats. She hoped she had left enough food for them to make it until she got back to the coast.

She had half expected that the buildings of the city would be crumbling and dead as well. But instead there was only evidence of lack of care. Windows were covered with dirt and film, weeds were growing thick in the cracks of the sidewalks, and nothing was lit.

The stoplights swinging lightly in the hot wind at the end of the overpass were now nothing more than dead eyes hanging over empty streets. It gave her the feeling that someone was watching her.

Carey shook off the feeling, took a second, long drink from the bottle of water, and stared down at the freeway. She had to be careful. There was no telling what waited for her there.

Damn she missed her cats.

The hot wind snapped at her short hair. At least now the winds didn't bring the smell of death as it had done the day she left. Four years of time had cleared that out, and she was grateful.

She picked up the backpack and shifted it slightly to make sure one strap didn't rub her shoulder too long. The pack contained enough water to get her by for a few days, plus food for two weeks, and extra ammunition for her rifle and the pistol in her belt.

She had spent a pretty good amount of time over the last two years learning how to fire that pistol and the rifle quickly and accurately. For some reason, she felt she actually might run into someone else alive on this hike. And since she was a woman alone, she didn't dare take any chances. But so far that hadn't been the case. Not even a sign that anyone had passed through the area at some point over the past four years.

Still, the small rifle felt good in her hands. A comfort. And for the rest of the walk into town she would carry it off her shoulder, loaded and ready.

Her hope, and her fear, was there *would* be other survivors in the city. She was convinced that a normal, sane person would have given up that hope by now; but still, here she was today, standing on the edge of the dead city, ready to check.

Carey sometimes lay awake at night listening to the waves pound the beach and rocks below her home and thought of people, and how nice it would be to talk to someone, or even listen to someone else talk. Just companionship. Four years of living alone had given her a lot of time to think, and she knew that simple, easy companionship wasn't going to happen. She was convinced she was going to die alone.

She glanced behind her, up the freeway the way she had come. Back that direction was home, with the comforts of generators for electricity, large screen television for running movies, and a converted neighbor's house full of more books than she would ever manage to read.

She couldn't believe that in all the death, she had managed to make the coast feel like home. The first year she had adopted two stray cats by slowly feeding them enough for them to trust her. Stingy was an old yellow cat who hogged the food, and Betty sat and purred while being petted, but never really left Stingy's side. Carey talked to them all the time.

She had also set up fishing nets and crab pots, and planned her days around finding enough food to keep going. During the spring, summer, and fall, she kept her gardens tended, with the biggest problem being keeping the deer out. She had built and stocked a root cellar, and filled another close-by house with canned goods she hoped would last.

Living like that, she had cut herself off from the sights, sounds, and reminders of what had happened to the rest of humanity. She knew how to be alone, how to live alone. That didn't worry her any more, since she had proven to herself she could do it. But for some reason the thought of *dying* alone scared her a great deal.

And she really wanted someone to talk to. Someone besides her cats. She had to find out if she really was alone, if the human race was going to die with her, or if there was still hope.

There had to be hope.

Considering the fluke circumstances that had allowed her to survive, she was certain that if there was anyone else, the numbers would be few. For a week before that last day, scientists around the world had been whispering among themselves about what seemed like a cloud approaching Earth, although actually Earth, and the rest of the solar system, were approaching the cloud.

No one was exactly certain what it was. Dust had been ruled out, with the leading theory being energy of some sort, visible only because of the light refraction it was causing to the stars on the other side.

Something out there was bending light, twisting it, ripping it apart, and Earth was going to pass right through that something. Even on the night side of the planet, no one would see the glow of the wave. It was just no big deal, just a scientific curiosity.

She had been a post-doc student in electromagnetics at the time, working at the University of Oregon with the renowned Dr. Addenson, the most famous man in her field. His main lab was down near the river in Portland, and she had taken an apartment in Portland, two hours north of the University of Oregon in Eugene, to work with him for the summer, and with luck, the fall semester. It had made being with her boyfriend, Sam, hard at times, since he was still in Eugene most of the time.

Dr. Addenson's belief was that Earth was about to flash through a low-level electromagnetic storm. It would take less than six seconds, by his calculations of the speed of the planet and the measurements they had managed to get of the cloud.

He had sent out a warning to others on his theory, to give them a chance to protect highly sensitive instruments. Strong electromagnetic pulses, like from an atomic blast, could shut down most modern equipment and destroy computers, but no one thought this wave was strong enough to do that.

Actually, no one knew what it was at all.

To prove his theory, Dr. Addenson designed an experiment with two dozen sets of sensitive electronic equipment, to monitor the effects of the pass-through. Part of the experiment was to have one set of control devices locked in a secure vault, designed to protect anything in it from any kind of electromagnetic pulse.

Carey had worked two long days and nights on the experiments, side-by-side with Addenson, getting them ready. Then, during the hour before the storm was to pass over, Dr. Addenson decided she should be closed in the vault along with the control-equipment to monitor them.

No one, not one scientist in the thousands who were aware of the cloud approaching, even thought it would be dangerous. So Carey didn't have any fear when she stepped into that vault and Dr. Addenson closed the door.

When she came out thirty minutes after the cloud had passed, Dr. Addenson lay dead on the floor.

It was a pure nightmare. It seemed that everyone had died in the midst of their normal activities.

The drivers of thousands of cars moving at all speeds had died instantly behind the wheels of their cars. The car wrecks were everywhere, clogging streets and smashed into buildings.

Out near the Portland airport dark clouds of smoke billowed into the air where some planes had crashed.

In an instant, the entire town had gone from a beautiful city to a nightmare filled with death.

Carey could barely remember stumbling out of the lab, checking for life in almost every body. She found Sam where she had left him that morning, still in her bed in her apartment.

Her mother was slumped over the sink of the family home in Beaverton, with the water still running. She had been preparing what looked like one of Carey's favorite meals, corned-beef and cabbage.

She had found her father in his office in the downtown area, slumped over his desk, his secretary slumped beside him.

Thousands and thousands of dead bodies, all seemingly caught in a moment in time. At first it seemed like a bad dream, then a nightmare she desperately wanted to wake up from.

Within hours it seemed the bodies started to smell, bloat up in the heat, look even more nightmarish as the maggots took over.

Finally, after two days of wandering around, Carey found herself back to the lab trying to discover what exactly had happened.

The instruments designed to record and test Dr. Addenson's theory told her the entire story of the storm passing over Earth. It had been electromagnetic, as Addenson had figured, but it had been resonating at the exact right band to shut down the human brain's electrical systems. All the signals that are constantly sent from the human brain to the heart and lungs were short-circuited.

In essence, people died before they even knew what had hit them. No one had been in pain, as far as Carey could tell, and no one had a chance to recover.

The storm's bandwidth had been very narrow. It had killed all dogs, but not small cats. She had discovered later that horses were gone, but not cattle. Rats, mice, most rodents were killed, but not most fish.

Deer had survived as well. And raccoons. And a lot of bees

and insects of different types. She had no idea of the long-term effects the massive disruptions in the food chains would have, and she really had no way of actually measuring why some animals' brains were short-circuited by the storm and others were not. All she knew was that humans had drawn the short straw.

After sitting beside Sam's rotting body and crying for a few hours the next morning, she had headed for the coast to get out of the growing smell and crammed city-of-death.

Now, four years later she was back.

Carey took another drink from the bottle of water, and studied the area in front of her. The freeway wound down the hill toward the main part of Portland that lay along the river. She could see most of the tall buildings, some of the riverfront, and all of the east side. Portland was still a beautiful town.

A few dozen cars were piled and scattered along the freeway where they had crashed when their occupants died. Wrecked cars was such a common sight for Carey, she often didn't even notice the bodies in them anymore. In these she could see the gleaming white of skeletons behind the steering wheels, their perpetual grins staring ahead.

She finished off the bottle of water, adjusted her backpack into place, and started off the overpass and down toward the empty, weed-littered freeway surface, her rifle in hand. Portland had been her home for a long time, a vibrant city she had loved.

Now she was back, and she had no idea what that would bring.

CHAPTER 2

He woke with a start as the alarm on the computer beeped loudly, echoing through his penthouse apartment. At first Toby Landel couldn't figure out exactly what he was hearing. He had been dreaming about waking up in the morning in his old college dorm room, to his old alarm clock, and the dream had morphed into a nightmarish feeling of the alarm clock going off forever while he searched and searched under piles of clothes and stacks of books, unable to find it no matter how hard he tried.

He had done that, in reality, more times than he wanted to remember back in those days, and now, eight years later, the dream of it still haunted him.

But the computer beeping sounded different, more intense than his old dorm alarm clock, and the reality of its high-pitched, quick beat slowly replaced the ringing in the dream.

He opened his eyes and stared at the white ceiling and wood beams over his head.

Something had triggered his security alarm again.

"Damn deer," he said, tossing aside the sheet and standing. He was nude, but since the morning seemed hot and bright, he didn't even bother to slip on his robe or slippers. He moved across the soft carpet toward the computer room, trying to push the sleep and the dream back completely. College was gone, his friends were gone, he was the only one left. And if he ever found that old alarm he'd smash it into a hundred pieces, just with the hopes that dream would stop.

Outside the expanse of open windows around him, the dead city of Portland looked exactly as it had every day for the past two years. But this morning the sun had already cleared off the haze, and he could tell without even going out that the air was hot and dry.

He had set up the penthouse apartment, on the fifteenth floor of what had been the Baxter Building, to cater to his every need. It had soft, rich carpet, big, expansive rooms, and an island kitchen in the center with bright lights and every appliance known to kitchens. He loved cooking, and used the kitchen almost more than any other area.

He had furnished the living room with a deep, comfortable recliner placed directly in front of a large screen television. He had also brought in a couch for the times he wanted to just lay down. To the right of the living room he had put together a weight and exercise room to keep his six-foot frame in top shape. He lifted every day, and ran on a treadmill facing the windows. He figured that he would never know when being in top shape would save his life.

Another recliner that matched the one in the living room, only because there had happened to be two of them in the furniture store the morning he had been looking, sat in front of a massive picture window that looked out over Portland and the Willamette River. Beyond the river and the east side of town he could see the snow-capped peak of Mt. Hood. He loved just sitting in that chair with a drink in his hand staring at the mountain.

Sometimes he sat there and read when it rained, watching the patterns of the water between chapters. When the world had been still alive, he never would have been able to afford a place like this. Now he figured he deserved it. Besides, who could tell him no?

The beeping continued, drawing him toward the computer room he had installed in the west corner of the big penthouse. He had been an electrician by craft before everyone had died, and had installed security cameras for a living for River Drive Security and Alarms. In fact, he had been installing a bank camera with his boss and two others the day everyone just died. He and Jenkins had been down in the vault when suddenly everything went silent on the comm link with the boss in the truck.

Jenkins had gone up to investigate, leaving Toby in the vault. Toby had never seen him again. By the time Toby had given up waiting, left the vault, and went to investigate, Jenkins was gone, and everyone else was dead. The only thing Toby could figure, in hindsight, was Jenkins had seen everyone dead, had freaked, and headed home to check on his wife and kids.

At first Toby thought that something airborne had killed everyone, and it would soon get him, so he had gone back inside. But after a short time of staring at dead bank customers and tellers, he knew that was stupid.

After that he had started to wander the streets, shocked at how people had died, staring at bodies, not really heading anywhere in particular for the first hour or so. Slowly it began to dawn on him that maybe he, and Jenkins, wherever he had gone, were the only ones left alive in a very large area.

Then, with one thought of his parents, it had become important to find out just how widespread this disaster had been.

His parents lived in Bend, a little resort city over the Cascade Mountains at the foot of Bachelor Ski Area. He had managed to make the six-hour drive to Bend in just under twelve, using six different cars when he came upon areas of the road that were jammed with wrecks. He had simply left the car and hiked until he found another car on the other side of the blockage.

All the way, he hoped they had been outside the influence of whatever it was that had happened, that he would find them alive and worried about him. As he got closer, the evidence told him that would not be the case.

He found his parents both dead, as well as everyone else in the small town. For an hour he had sat in the middle of the main intersection, with the light changing from green to red over his head, honking a car's horn. The sound seemed impossibly loud, echoing off the buildings and the pine-covered mountains.

No one came and told him to stop.

He knew he was alone. Really alone, and the thought scared him more than he had ever been scared before.

The next few days were a blur. He had somehow managed to bury his parents next to his grandparents in the town's cemetery. Then he had gone down to his favorite bar and dragged all the bodies out onto the sidewalk and sat them at tables he had put there, posing each body as best he could in positions of drinking.

Then he had gone inside, alone, and filled the top of the bar with bottles of booze.. That day, and for days after, he had gotten so drunk he couldn't think.

It was finally the smell of rotting human bodies that had driven him away from the small town and out into a cabin way up in the Cascade Mountains, where he stayed for a long winter, waiting for nature to clean up the mess.

Then for a year he had wandered the Northwest, looking for anyone else alive, returning to Portland two years ago.

The computer alarm kept beeping, getting louder as he entered the room.

"All right, all right," he said, "I'm coming."

He expected to see nothing on the monitor, and to have to rewind a tape to see what had triggered the alarm. He had set up the system of motion detectors two years ago, using sensors that triggered cameras and ran off of batteries that he recharged every six months. He had installed the system when he realized the lights from the generator running his penthouse apartment could be seen for miles around the city. Most of the power had failed in the metro area, so his place stood out like a beacon at night.

And if anyone else was alive out there, he figured it would be better to know when they were getting close. The cameras, waiting with their motion detectors, guarded over twenty different ways into the city. About five times a week, deer triggered the alarms. But once, six months before, a ragged, insane-looking man with machine guns had come through, heading north.

The guy clearly did not bathe often, was dragging a pack in a wagon, and talked to himself constantly. No matter how much Toby had wanted another human back in his life, he couldn't bring himself to talk to the guy. The man was just too dangerous. Toby had watched him for two days with hidden cameras, but never let the guy know he was around.

The guy had done one good thing for Toby. He had proven that there were others out there, alive and surviving in some fashion. And ever since that day, Toby had been trying to figure out where they would be. He didn't know what had killed everyone, but something about being inside that bank vault had saved him. And if it had saved him, it had saved others, he was sure.

"All right," he said, dropping his nude body into the chair in front of his monitor command screens. The first thing he did was punch off the beeping alarm. Then he glanced at the control board. The motion had been on the old Interstate 5 headed south. Deer often went through there, since that area was between the hills and the river.

He flicked up an image from a camera he had hidden on a pole, expecting to see either deer, or nothing at all. The sight of a woman, standing on an overpass, shocked him to his very core.

His fingers fumbled over the controls for a moment before he brought up the zoom.

A woman, by herself.

He wasn't seeing things. She wore a black, sleeveless T-shirt, jeans, and tennis shoes. She had short, brown hair, light skin, and a clearly muscled body. He couldn't take his gaze off of her. In the last two years he would have never expected to see a woman, let alone a beautiful woman.

He stared at her image as she finished putting lotion on her arms and then took a drink of water. He would have been attracted to her even when everyone was still alive. He had kept the idea of ever meeting a woman again so tucked away in his mind, he wasn't sure yet if he was still dreaming.

As he watched, she headed off the overpass, a small rifle in her hand, walking with the assured gait of someone who had confidence to spare.

He wanted to shout at the screen that he was here, that she should wait.

It took only a moment before she was headed down the freeway toward town and out of his camera range.

The moment she disappeared he felt a jolt of panic go through him. "Oh, damn," he said.

His hands scrambled over the massive control board he had set up for the security cameras. Finally he managed to activate the next camera covering a section of the old Interstate

5 south of town. For a long moment he thought he had lost her, then she came around a large pile of wrecked cars and kept walking, right at him, as the motion-sensor alarm for that area started to ring.

She was too good to be true, an impossible dream.

He flipped off the alarm, sitting back in silence as he watched her stride toward him.

This could not be happening.

Almost the entire population of the planet seemed to be dead, yet here was a woman walking right into his life.

And just like back in his college days, he had no idea how to meet her.

The rifle carried with ease in her hands seemed to grow bigger.

At least back in college, trying to meet a girl didn't mean risking getting shot. But as he stared at this woman's face, he had no doubt that was a risk he was going to have to take.

CHAPTER 3

Carey kept her pace slow and easy in the hot sun as she headed down the freeway, moving in and around wrecked cars with their drivers still strapped behind the wheels, smiling sickly, skeleton-smiles at her.

She didn't let herself look inside the cars too much, because even after four years, those faces still seemed too human, too lifelike in their final poses. Especially the skeletons and mummified remains of the children, strapped in car seats, trusting their parents to take care of them. She didn't want to think about having children. At one point in her life she had thought she might like it. Now that thought wasn't allowed to the surface of her mind.

She stared ahead at the big overpass and the signs directing traffic to the downtown area, or along the bridge and beyond to Seattle.

Seattle. Wow, that seemed so far away. Maybe if there was no one alive here that she could talk to, she could take a look in Seattle some day?

Maybe.

Right now that seemed too far, too much to think about.

She made herself focus on the city in front of her. It seemed so familiar, yet so alien, especially walking along the freeway to get into town. She found herself staying to the road's edge, not that she needed to, just out of respect for old habits.

Ahead of her a half mile or so, the Marriott Hotel tower rose over the river. Her plan was to stay there, in one of the unoccupied rooms with a view. When working in town she had never had a reason, or enough money, to stay in such a nice place. It would be a treat.

She would find a good room, set it up as a base for exploring around the city, and maybe, if she had enough nerve to see Sam's body again, go back to her old apartment for some keepsakes. She planned on stocking the hotel room with food, maybe even get a portable generator in for electricity. But before anything, she would have to check the water, to make sure the water tanks of a place like that had enough good water to last her for a time. After a day this hot, she was going to need a shower.

Maybe with a little work, she could even make the place permanent. It hadn't occurred to her until just that moment that she could have a place in the city, a place on the coast, a place just about anywhere in the world she wanted.

Nothing was stopping her.

She moved along the off-ramp that led down to Front

Street and then along the river front a dozen more blocks to the hotel. The grass along the river had turned to weeds, the sidewalks and streets were cracked and growing grass in places. But the city still had a beauty about it, with the blue river flowing through it, the mountains around it, and the green trees everywhere.

The air smelled faintly of water and fish, and birds chirped and flitted from nests in the branches of the trees along the old park. She could see where birds had stained the edges of buildings, building nests in windows. Even though it was hot, she was lucky she had come into town on such a beautiful day.

Two blocks short of the hotel, something moved out of the corner of her eye. She snapped around, the rifle up and aimed, her blood racing.

A bird flittered away. She sighed and lowered the gun. "All right," she said out loud, "Calm down, and don't go shooting every little thing that moves."

"I'm very glad to hear you say that," a deep, rich voice said to her right.

She spun around, the rifle again up, her heart pounding so hard she thought it was going to jump right out of her chest.

She found herself face-to-face with a man about her age, with brown, unruly hair, twinkling brown eyes, and a large smile. He had his hands in the air like he had just been caught robbing a bank. He had stepped out of the shadows near an office building and was no more than ten steps from her.

He wore a plain white T-shirt, jeans and new-looking tennis shoes. He had the appearance of having dressed quickly, yet still seemed together and clean. He was also one of the best-looking men she had ever seen, even before everyone died.

It was as if time in the dead city around them froze.

Nothing on the street moved. The river sounds seemed to drop back to silence. She didn't even feel the heat.

She kept her gaze locked on his, the rifle pointed at his chest. She had hoped to find someone else alive, but she hadn't really expected to. And she had never expected to find someone so damn good-looking, and her age.

"I'm not going to bite," the guy said, smiling. His voice was deep and rich and matched his rugged face. His voice stayed level and didn't shake, even though she could tell he was worried about her shooting him.

Then he laughed. "Sorry for the cliché. I didn't know what else to say. I am unarmed and alone. In fact, until you showed up, I thought I *was* alone. Period."

Carey didn't lower her gun, and he didn't lower his arms. She had to get her wits about her, really find out who this person was, and what she had just walked into.

"How did you know I was here?"

"Security cameras," he said, pointing up at the top of a pole back down Front Street. "I have them on all the main entrances into town. A person living alone can never be too careful. But, to be honest, I was also hoping to find someone else alive, passing through."

"And you sit all day and watch your cameras?" she asked, now even more worried that she had run into a weirdo. Why hadn't she listened to her little voice when she felt she was being watched? Mistakes like that could get her killed.

He laughed. "Not hardly. In fact, you woke me when you stopped on the overpass. I have motion detector alarms."

She could feel herself starting to relax just a little, and her little voice wasn't screaming that this man was dangerous. She would have set up security cameras like that if she had thought of it, or known how.

She forced herself to think, slowly, giving herself time to calm down. One mistake, one slip, and she could find herself in a very bad situation. He was shorter than Sam had been, but still clearly very strong. She had to be careful, no matter how much she just wanted to lower her gun and hug this stranger and just talk to him.

"So where do you live?" she asked.

"Baxter Building," he said. "Been there for two years, in the Penthouse. How about you?"

"On the coast," she said.

He nodded, as if understanding that. "Yeah, I was up in the Cascades, in the forest, until the smell cleared."

"How did you survive?"

"Doing the security system in a bank in Beaverton. I was down in the vault, but I have no idea why that protected me."

"I do," she said.

At that his eyes lit up, and his arms lowered a little. "You do? Why? If you know that, it would help me figure out where there are more people alive."

Carey took a deep breath and ignored his question for a moment. Clearly, if he had been watching her, he had known she had a rifle, had known she would get the drop on him, and had risked being shot by introducing himself. The guy had courage, and really wanted her to trust him.

She motioned that he should lower his arms, and she lowered the rifle, keeping her hand on the trigger and the rifle ready to bring up quickly.

"Thanks," he said. He moved his shoulders around a few times. "I clearly need more reps on those hand-raising isometrics."

She smiled, and he smiled back.

How could the first man she had seen alive in four years have such a wonderful smile?

"So, do you have a name?" she asked.

"Toby," he said. "Toby Landel. An actual, native Oregonian, born and raised."

She actually laughed at that, since something like that mattered only to Oregonians.

"I'm Carissa Noack. People used to call me Carey. Also a native through and through."

It felt strange using her full name after four years. Strange, and yet somehow, normal, as if having and using a full name returned a little civilization to the world.

"How about I cook us both breakfast?" Toby said. "My stomach is starting to sound like an earthquake, and I bet you haven't had a good omelet since you left the coast."

"Omelet?" she asked, the word out of her mouth before she had a chance to stop it. She hadn't had anything like a real egg since she moved to the coast. On the hike in she had seen chickens, but hadn't been able to get close to any.

"Yeah, real eggs and everything," he said. "Honest."

"How? Here in the city?"

He nodded, smiling as if he was very proud of having eggs. "It seems chickens survived whatever killed everyone. So I went out into the country and trapped a few, including a couple of roosters, and set them loose in the Rose Garden."

"You're kidding?" she asked. The Rose Garden was the big basketball arena where the Portland Trailblazers basketball team had played.

"I'm not," he said, laughing again. "It does seem strange, now that I think of it. I just figured the seats would make great nests for them, plus it's big enough to hold a lot of birds."

She laughed at the idea. The Rose Garden as a chicken coop. How perfect. "What do you feed them? How many do you have?"

He shrugged. "Every few weeks I scatter a truckload of grain from some sacks I found in a warehouse down by the river. Every month or so I trap some more birds and turn them loose in there. The population seems to be growing. I try to go get the eggs I can find every few days, but there are always more than I can use. I take a bird every few weeks for a special dinner. I bet I have five hundred birds in there now, if not more."

"Amazing," she said.

"Thanks," he said, smiling. "I'd be glad to show it to you, right after breakfast. I would love to have someone to talk to while I'm cooking after all these years."

She stared at him for a moment. She had come back into town with the hope of finding someone else still alive. Now she had, and she didn't know what to do. She hadn't expected this, she hadn't expected anyone, let alone a great-looking guy who raised chickens and could cook.

"All right, Mr. Toby Landel," she said, swinging her rifle up on her shoulder, but making sure her pistol was within easy and quick reach in her belt, "let's just go see how good a cook you really are."

The smile that lit up his face almost melted her right there in the street. She had so wanted company, been so lonely for simply talking to another human, and clearly he had been the same way.

He indicated that they should head off down Front Street in the direction she had been heading. She knew the Baxter Building was beyond the Marriott Hotel a few blocks, so he was indicating the right direction.

She moved into a position beside him, matching him stride-for-stride, feeling just like a junior-high girl faced with talking to a boy on a first date.

She had no idea what to talk about, and in this case, she hoped he didn't turn out to be crazy. Actually, she had worried about that with boys in junior-high as well, so nothing seemed that different, except that they were the only two people left alive in the city, and if he threatened her, she would have to kill him.

CHAPTER 4

It had gone better than Toby had hoped. She hadn't shot him. On top of that, she had actually accepted his invitation to breakfast, after a little bit of conversation.

It was also a fact that his cameras had not done her justice. Up close, her deep brown eyes and intense gaze melted him like no other woman had ever done before. Now granted, he hadn't seen a live woman in four years, but she would have had that effect on him before everyone died.

Now all he wanted to do was talk with her. He had not realized until he started speaking just how much he had missed interacting with humans.

"This is the place," he said, his arm sweeping around the penthouse that no one had seen but him in four years. "And that's Buddy."

Buddy was the big, gray-and-white cat that had adopted him when he moved into this building. Buddy hated going out, loved sitting with him while he read, and was a great companion.

Buddy walked up to Carey as she knelt down to pet him. "I've got two. Stingy and Betty."

"I bet you miss them," Toby said. "How long have you been gone?"

"Eight days," she said, petting Buddy as Toby went into the kitchen area and opened the refrigerator. He got out the eggs and some fixings to go in the eggs.

She stood and dropped her pack, putting her rifle on top of it. Then she moved over and looked at his kitchen. "Wow, you have everything in here."

"The advantage of not having to pay for anything," he said. "Feel free to look around as I get this started. The computer monitor room is up front in the corner, bathroom is back there on the left."

He watched as she hesitated, then decided to go ahead and look at his place. She poked her head into the computer room, then nodded. "You are good at electronics, aren't you?"

"Not as good as I used to be when I worked with it every day," he said, breaking six eggs into a pan. "I'm afraid my omelets are basically eggs mixed with green peppers and onions from my rooftop garden, and some canned ham. I haven't had the courage to try any mushrooms."

"That sounds wonderful," she said, smiling at him as she ran her hand across the back of the chair he had facing the window. "This is some view."

"No one seemed to be using the place, so I figured why not," he said.

"Know that feeling," she said, smiling. "I'm using three different houses on the coast."

Silence filled the room, broken only by the sound of his fork stirring the eggs, and his knife cutting the pepper.

Finally she moved back over to the edge of the kitchen island and leaned on the counter. "You know, for four years I've been hoping to find someone alive, have someone to talk to; and now that we have met, I don't know what to say."

Toby stopped cutting and looked at her, letting himself be drawn into her deep, brown eyes. "I'm feeling the same way, to be honest. Like a high-school kid afraid to talk to the girl in the chair beside him."

She laughed. "I'm feeling more junior-high."

"I didn't notice girls back then," he said. "I didn't start paying attention to them until sophomore year."

For some reason that admission seemed to break the ice. He could feel it, and the sound of her light laugh filled the room.

As he cooked, they went through their backgrounds, his in Bend, hers in Beaverton. He had been a year behind her in school, and for some reason, even though they were both at the University of Oregon at the same time, they had no memory of seeing each other.

Over breakfast, which she ate without hesitation, they talked about their families.

When they were done eating, and he had refused to let her help clean up, she asked if she could use his bathroom. When he agreed, and warned her about the hot water being a little too hot, she had smiled like he had given her a perfect Christmas present.

As she was taking her shower, Toby took a cup of coffee and moved over to his chair in front of the window. How had he managed to actually meet another person, let alone a woman he was attracted to, and that he enjoyed talking with?

Had he dreamed the entire thing? Was the water running in the bathroom just his mind playing tricks on him?

And what was he going to do next?

Actually—more importantly—what was *she* going to do next?

CHAPTER 5

By the time Carey finished with the most heavenly-feeling shower she could remember in years, her mind had cleared some. She was still having a hard time believing that anyone else was left alive, let alone someone nice. But unless she was dreaming this shower and that fantastic omelet, Toby was actually out there.

She put on clean clothes, stuffed the dirty ones in her pack, put her pistol back in her belt and went out, dropping her pack beside the door before petting Buddy.

"Everything all right?" he asked from a big lounge chair half facing one of the floor-to-ceiling windows.

"Perfect," she said. "I haven't had a hot shower since I left home. Thank you."

"No problem," he said. "There is coffee on the counter in the big pot. Help yourself."

He suddenly jumped up, moved into the living room, and

dragged the other matching chair back so that it sat at an angle, facing the window. Carey poured herself a cup of wonderful-smelling coffee and joined him.

"Sorry," he said, smiling at her as he finished getting the second chair in place beside the first. "Just not used to having guests."

She sat and put her feet up. "I know the feeling."

She enjoyed the silence and the fantastic view for a few moments. Then he asked, "You said you knew what caused all this?"

"I do."

"Would you tell me?" he asked, a look of hope in his intelligent eyes.

She sipped the cup of coffee and then smiled at him. "For a wonderful breakfast, a hot shower, and this cup of coffee, it seems I can do that."

He laughed and she started into a description about her old job, what she had been doing when everyone died, and what had caused it.

"Electromagnetic pulse?" he asked when she finished.

"Basically, yes," she said. "Just very weak, and at such an exact wavelength as to short out some animal brains, including humans. I was protected by the experiment vault; you must have been protected in the bank."

Toby jumped up and started pacing.

Carey sat and watched him move. Just doing something as simple as watching another human move was a joy.

"Do you know what this means?" he said, the excitement clear.

"No, what?"

"That there has to be others alive out there besides us. Maybe even an entire community of people. Maybe more than one community, in touch with others around the world."

"You're not making sense," she said. "Where? And how?"

"Cheyenne Mountain in Colorado, for one," he said. "There are lots and lots of people who work down in that mountain twenty-four hours a day. It's protected from electromagnetic pulses like we were, and they all would have survived."

She remembered reading stories of how Cheyenne Mountain was built to withstand a direct atomic hit. There would be people alive in there.

"And there were places like that under the White House, and on other military bases," he said. "And atomic subs were protected. If it's electromagnetic pulses that did this, then there will be lots of people alive out there. And they will gather in groups. All we need to do is find them."

He dropped into his chair and sat staring over the hot city.

Carey looked at him, then sat back as well, letting the idea that he had just given her sink in. She knew he was right. Suddenly the world on the other side of those windows didn't seem so dead.

Or so hopeless.

He was right, there were other people out there, somewhere, maybe trying to rebuild civilization. She had skills that she could offer them.

So did Toby, if that computer surveillance room was any indication.

"I am very, very glad you decided to come back to the city," he said, looking at her. "And that you didn't shoot me on sight."

"So am I," she said, smiling at him.

He turned to look over the city.

They both sat, silently, staring at the river and the mountains to the east. She had never felt so comfortable in a silence.

And now the silence wasn't because of death, but because of the chance of life. It was a silence of two people thinking. And what kept going over and over in her mind was that now, maybe there was a chance she wouldn't die alone.

After what seemed like a very long time, Toby asked, "Want to go with me? See who we can find? Between the two of us, we can figure out where to look."

She stared into his eyes. She could see hope. And she could see trust. Without a doubt she wanted to go look for others with him. "I'd have to go get my cats," she said.

He smiled. "I think Buddy and I can help with that."

"Then the answer is yes," she said. "Let's go see who we can find."

"It's a long way to Colorado," he said.

"It's been a long four years for both of us," she said, reaching over and taking his firm hand in hers, enjoying the feel of his skin against hers. "I think we can make it."

He gently squeezed her hand and smiled. "So do I."

A MATTER FOR A FUTURE YEAR

A SEEDERS UNIVERSE SHORT STORY

INTRODUCTION

A single Seeder scout ship trapped on the edge of a distant, uncharted galaxy. Chairman Peter German holds the fate of the three thousand people on the Pale Light.

Main drives mysteriously not working, the ship hobbles along at sub-light speed with not enough supplies to reach the nearest Earth-like planet

The Chairman faces a hard, hard choice. He must find the solution.

Galaxy spanning ships, billions of civilizations, the Seeders Universe stories and novels cover it all. But "A Matter for a Future Year" brings it all down to a single human choice. And the price paid by those who risk to explore outward.

CHAPTER 1

It's not going to work," Davis said, staring at the control panel in front of him.

The silence in the massive control room felt like a weight on Chairman Peter German, pressing down on his chest. Twenty officers still pretended to study their stations, but all of them were waiting for his response. He knew that.

He glanced at Davis, his best friend and third in command. Davis was bald and liked to wear T-shirts. Davis only shrugged an apology at the answer.

German could sense the growing frustration, anger, and even hints of panic in his command bridge crew. He felt the same emotions exactly.

German stood six feet tall, had striking black hair that trailed over his collar, and dark green eyes that people said felt like he could look through them. No one had ever questioned his ability to lead and no one was now either. In fact, they were depending on his leadership.

He wore tan slacks, an open-neck dress shirt, and tennis shoes. After centuries on this ship, uniforms were a forgotten thing of the past for everyone.

In situations like this, he never sat down, but instead either stood by his own chair so he could see his panels, or roamed around the bridge.

In his seven hundred years of being a Chairman of the Seeder's scout ship *Pale Light,* he had never felt so bad, so lost, or so flat confused as he did right now. But he sure couldn't show that or admit that to his bridge crew. Over eighty thousand people on this ship depended on him and his bridge crew to find a solution.

So they would find one.

Pale Light and everyone on board had all made a great living for centuries. All Seeder ships ran like a corporation, which was why he was called Chairman. On top of that, he had gotten the original funding for the ship and had the most shares in the corporation. Over the centuries, they had taken many lucrative contracts to scout galaxies ahead of the wave of Seeder ships.

At the moment they were twenty galaxies out ahead of the front wave. It would take the front wave of Seeder ships over two hundred thousand years to work their way here, and that was because most of the galaxies between here and the main wave were small.

Pale Light, with him in charge, had explored uncounted galaxies, had even discovered two young alien races in different galaxies and seen remnants of three other alien races in three other galaxies. Everyone on board got bonuses when they found aliens and warned the Seeder ships in the main wave away from those galaxies.

Now *Pale Light* had a problem.

Everyone on board had a problem.

They were dead in space. And not a person on the ship had any idea why or what was wrong.

They had suddenly dropped out of drive at a dead stop. That should not have been possible either, but it had happened.

And unless they solved this problem in short order, he would have to start putting most of the people on board into suspended animation, something that had never been done on *Pale Light* since it was built.

He had already given the order to start checking the chambers and preparing them.

Pale Light just didn't have enough supplies on board to feed all eighty thousand people for the five-year sub-light trip to the nearest inhabitable planet.

And even when they got there, they would be stuck on a single planet in a galaxy with nothing more than a number designation and no hope of anyone even looking for them for two or three hundred years.

He could smell the sweat of the officers around him, many who had served with him for centuries. They all knew that scouting into other galaxies was a dangerous mission. Many Seeder scout ships like the *Pale Light* had gone missing over the centuries. That's why they had been paid so well. But after centuries, he had forgotten the danger.

They all had.

Now the reason they had been paid so much faced them.

He glanced around at his top bridge crew. All of them needed a break from the bridge, him included. They had been working on what had happened and different solutions to what was wrong with *Pale Light* and the future that faced them for over five hours straight.

There had to be a solution, a reason for the sudden stop. But none of them could find it yet.

Pale Light should be working fine. It was not.

It was that simple.

The reason why was the main problem as far as he was concerned.

And the second problem was what to do about it.

And about the eighty thousand people who worked for him.

They had less than twenty-four hours by everyone's calculation before he would have to order most of the population of *Pale Light* into the suspension chambers to give a skeleton crew enough supplies to make it the five years of sub-light travel.

He did not want to do that because he understood, just as everyone on this bridge understood, that just under one percent of the humans going into suspended animation did not wake up.

That meant that the moment he gave that order, he was sentencing a lot of people who worked for him to their death.

But if he didn't order it, they would all starve in a matter of months.

He ran his fingers through his black hair, then took a deep breath and said to the bridge crew. "We get some food, some showers, mandatory for all of us, and some rest. We return here in six hours, rested, cleaned up and ready to solve this. Get the evening crew to take over until then."

With that, German teleported to his cabin.

He loved his four-room suite. He had decorated the rooms in soft browns, with soft brown furniture, warm, comfortable tan floors, and wood-toned tables and countertops.

His fiancée, Dr. Kathy Spears, had helped him. A couple times he had tried to get her to join him on the *Pale Light,* but she had wanted to stay in her practice for a few more years.

They talked almost every night and since *Pale Light* reported back every two years, they reconnected then and spent six months together. One of these times, she would join him. She had promised. But as she said, they had lots of time.

He picked up the holo-image of Kathy on his bedroom nightstand, then put it back down again.

He couldn't think about her right now and he didn't dare allow himself to even think about the problem. He needed some rest. He stripped off his clothes and climbed into his shower. Ten minutes later, feeling slightly refreshed, he put on fresh clothes and went into his kitchen to fix himself a sandwich.

After eating half the turkey sandwich and drinking a glass of fruit juice, he was ready for a nap.

There was a solution. He knew that. They just had to find it.

And find out why this had happened in the first place.

Rest would help.

He cleared his mind, lay down on the bed, and was asleep almost instantly.

Centuries of practice clearing ship's business from his mind before sleeping allowed him to do that.

Even dire problems.

CHAPTER 2

Chairman Peter German woke three hours later, feeling much better.

He washed off his face, once again changed to a clean shirt, and went back to the kitchen to finish the other half of the turkey sandwich he had made earlier.

As he ate, he pulled up some of the data they had worked out earlier.

If a support crew was going to have enough food to survive a five-year sub-light trip to the nearest planet that would sustain a human population, he had to order all but three hundred of the eighty thousand on board into suspended animation. They would lose around five hundred people if he did that, but the rest would survive.

Sub-light drives worked, but something had blocked the *Pale Light's* hyper drives. Everything showed fine on all engine readings, just something stopped the ship from jumping.

It was as if hyper space, real space, and everything else around them had just stopped existing.

They had done every reading of the empty space around them that they could and some that no one had even tried in centuries. Nothing was there.

Nothing.

Empty space surrounded them.

But he and all the scientists on board knew that empty space, really, truly empty space did not exist. Space was always full of so many things. But it seemed empty space actually did exist and they were parked solidly in the middle of a large bubble of it.

With that, he went to his private research computer in his office. That computer gave him access to many confidential reports in the Seeder's network and command structure that had been stored on board and updated every time they returned to the leading edge with their reports. He was the only one on board that had access to the confidential files, although if something happened to him, Rose Marie, his second in command, knew where they were and how to get into them.

He looked up the reference to "empty space" to see if other ships had run into this kind of thing before.

What he found scared him more than the idea of putting almost everyone who worked for him into suspended animation.

It seemed that major studies, all highly classified, had been done on Empty Space or Void Space as it was called. It seemed that nothing existed in the space, including time.

Empty Space was basically a void in time and space. The voids were small and no one in his main records had figured out how they were formed. But it had a very real warning. If caught by one, get out quickly.

Another scientist called Empty Space the only reliable time travel machine into the future in the universe.

"Oh, shit," German said, his stomach twisting down on the turkey sandwich he had just finished.

He touched a button on his wall. "All command crew return at once to the bridge."

He instantly teleported there.

A young man by the name of Moore was at the helm. He had a head of bright red hair and freckles. He usually only saw duty in the night shift.

"Moore," German said, "ease sub-light drive up to full at once."

Moore nodded and focused on his panel.

German turned to his second in command, Rose Marie, who had just appeared on the bridge. Her short brown hair was still wet and she looked as if she had missed a button in getting her light blue blouse on in a rush.

"Head us toward that planet we found earlier that's five years out," German said to her and she nodded and stepped to navigation.

German turned back to Moore. "We at full speed yet?"

"We are, sir," Moore said. "Eighty percent of light."

"Then push it harder."

"But…" Moore started to say.

German nodded. "I know all about time issues at sub-light.

Just do it. I want this ship going at 95 percent of light speed as soon as you can get it worked up there. When we get out we'll reset all the clocks."

Moore only nodded and turned back to his controls.

Davis was now back at his panel, so German turned to his friend, "How far to the edge of Empty Space?"

"At 95 percent of light, we should get there in twenty-two hours."

German took a deep breath. That was a very, very long time.

Maybe too long.

"Davis, Rose Marie, I need you both in my cabin in ten minutes."

With that he jumped back to his cabin suite, got himself a glass of apricot juice, and dropped onto his couch in his living room. There was an image of Kathy on the end table.

He reached over and turned the image off.

He would let Rose Marie and Davis look at the classified files on the studies of Empty Space when they got here. And then they could talk about it.

And decide exactly what to do or not do.

But now he knew why Seeder Scout Ships vanished at times.

Empty Space.

They didn't vanish. They just took a trip into the future.

How far into the future was now the question.

CHAPTER 3

Chairman Peter German stood beside Davis and watched the screens around the large bridge. So far nothing on long-range sensors had changed. The small galaxy they had been exploring when trapped by Empty Space had not changed at all.

"Ten seconds to the edge," Rose Marie said, moving over to stand on the other side of German from Davis.

They had no idea what would happen when they crossed over that edge.

Or if Empty Space would even let them leave. There just hadn't been enough data in those classified files to help them even begin to make an educated guess.

But German was betting that once outside the confines of the Empty Space bubble, *Pale Light* would work just fine. At least he hoped it would. Because if it didn't, he would have to order most of the employees on board into animation.

"Now!" Davis said as the *Pale Light* went through the edge of the Empty Space bubble.

Everything changed.

As German had feared, the universe they had left when they entered Empty Space was not the same universe they had returned to.

There were gasps from around the bridge.

"Not possible," one person said.

German wanted to say "Very possible." But didn't.

"Get us away from that thing a ways and slow us down," German said to navigation. His concern right now was not what had happened to the outside world, but to what was happening inside *Pale Light*.

Davis was ahead in the thought. He turned to engineering. "Are standard drives working?"

"They are," Flame said from his panel, almost bouncing in excitement.

"Jump us a few light years away from that Empty Space and come to full stop," German said. "Then I want reports."

But German knew what he was seeing on the screens. The galaxy they were in had already been seeded and was a good hundred thousand years into development.

The front wave of the Seeder Ships had gotten here and passed right by them.

They had been inside that small bubble for at least three hundred thousand years.

"Find the front line of the seeding ships," German said, turning to Rose Marie.

She nodded and went back to her station.

German stood there, just staring at the inhabited galaxy they had been scouting. He never went back into the galaxies after seeding. He knew that millions of Seeders stayed behind to guild the seeded human cultures up to maturity. But he had never been one of them.

He always liked being out ahead of the crowds.

Seeing a galaxy alive with human life just felt odd to him. Galaxies he explored never had anything more than lower animal life. If that.

Rose Marie came back and stood beside German and Davis as they both stared at the screens and the data and reports starting to pour in from all the stations around the ship.

"The front line is working about ten galaxies beyond this one," Rose Marie said. "About a four-month trip at normal speeds."

"We were in Empty Space for three hundred and twenty-one thousand years," Davis said. "The people on board with families back on the old front line are going to have problems."

German nodded. "Get the counseling services warned."

He didn't let himself think about Kathy.

Davis moved to get that started.

"So now what do we do?" Rose Marie asked, her voice almost a whisper, as if talking to herself.

"The same thing we have always done," German said without looking away from all the reports flowing in. "We go back to command, get paid, and get back to work."

"Think we have back pay waiting for us?" Davis asked as he rejoined them.

German laughed. "This might be a very rich ship by the time we go back out again."

"Three hundred thousand years of progress," Rose Marie said. "This ship might be very dated."

German shook his head. "I doubt it will be. Seeders don't invent new things very often. We just explore and keep moving forward and giving human life to every planet we can find."

"Ain't that the truth," Davis said.

German turned to Rose Marie. "Get us to command. We have some reports to file and back pay to collect."

She nodded and with that he teleported back to his suite. Then, with a quick search through the Seeder database, he discovered what had happened to Kathy.

Five years after he and *Pale Light* had vanished without a trace, she married another doctor.

Three hundred and ten years later, while on a rescue mission to a small moon, she died in a ship crash.

He went into his bedroom, took her holo-image cube from his nightstand, then went into the living room and took her picture from there and put both cubes in a drawer.

And as he closed the drawer over her, he said simply, "Sorry."

Then he squared his shoulders and teleported back to the bridge. He had a business to run, eighty thousand people on board to help get through this. He would grieve for Kathy later.

Much later.

He had a job to do first.

NEWSLETTER SIGN-UP

Follow Dean on BookBub

Be the first to know!

Just sign up for the Dean Wesley Smith newsletter, and keep up with the latest news, releases and so much more—even the occasional giveaway. So, what are you waiting for? To sign up go to deanwesleysmith.com.

But wait! There's more. Sign up for the WMG Publishing newsletter, too, and get the latest news and releases from all of the WMG authors and lines, including Kristine Kathryn Rusch, Kristine Grayson, Kris Nelscott, *Pulphouse Fiction Magazine, Smith's Monthly*, and so much more.

To sign up go to wmgpublishing.com.

ABOUT THE AUTHOR

Considered one of the most prolific writers working in modern fiction, *USA Today* bestselling writer Dean Wesley Smith published far more than a hundred novels in forty years, and hundreds of short stories across many genres.

At the moment he produces novels in several major series, including the time travel Thunder Mountain novels set in the Old West, the galaxy-spanning Seeders Universe series, the urban fantasy Ghost of a Chance series, a superhero series starring Poker Boy, and a mystery series featuring the retired detectives of the Cold Poker Gang.

His monthly magazine, *Smith's Monthly*, which consists of only his own fiction, premiered in October 2013 and offers readers more than 70,000 words per issue, including a new and original novel every month.

During his career, Dean also wrote a couple dozen *Star Trek* novels, the only two original *Men in Black* novels, Spider-Man and X-Men novels, plus novels set in gaming and television worlds. Writing with his wife Kristine Kathryn Rusch under the name Kathryn Wesley, he wrote the novel for the NBC miniseries The Tenth Kingdom and other books for *Hallmark Hall of Fame* movies.

He wrote novels under dozens of pen names in the worlds of comic books and movies, including novelizations of almost a dozen films, from *The Final Fantasy* to *Steel* to *Rundown.*

Dean also worked as a fiction editor off and on, starting at Pulphouse Publishing, then at *VB Tech Journal,* then Pocket Books, and now at WMG Publishing, where he and Kristine Kathryn Rusch serve as series editors for the acclaimed *Fiction River* anthology series.

For more information about Dean's books and ongoing projects, go to his website at www.deanwesleysmith.com and sign up for his newsletter.

For more information:

www.deanwesleysmith.com

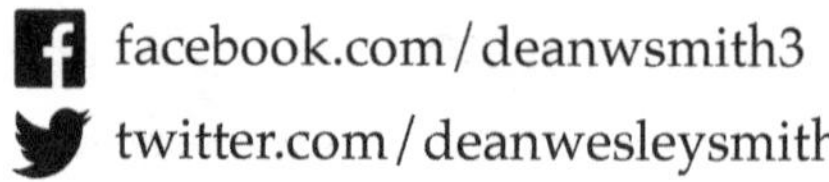